PUM PUM

Queen of the wind-up,
with mad sex appeal

FROM THE PEN OF *Ni'cola*

PUBLISHER'S NOTE:

*This book is a work of fiction. Names, Characters, Places,
and incidents either are products of the author's
imagination or are used fictitiously. Any resemblance to
actual events or locales or persons, living or dead, is
pure and entirely coincidental.*

Pum Pum
Written by: Ni'cola Mitchell
Edited by: Keyoka Kinzy, Andre Eaton
Text Formation: Write on Promotions
Cover Design and Layout: TSP
Printed in the United States of America

From the pen of Ni'cola

Being a Jamaican national, but growing up in the United States, I always felt out of place. Whenever we went back home to Jamaica, my family members would say that I chat like a Yankee (spoke like an American) and was a fake Yaude... In America, especially the West Side of Las Vegas (the hood), where back in the 80's there were very few West Indian people. My friends and their parents would shun almost everything about my heritage. From the food we ate, the way that we spoke, to the way I could wind my hips when I danced. The constant ridicule made me embarrassed of my roots, my upbringings. It made me hate it whenever my mother would blast the Calypso music from the floor model stereo in our living room and my stepfather would stand in the doorway dancing for our neighbors. I began hating who I was and practiced to speak *American* and tried to become someone that I was not.

I felt like no one understood me except my best friend Steevie Washington. He embraced my culture with open arms and would come over and dance and learned how to chat Jamaican Patois, a dialect that is also known as Jamaican Creole by linguists. (It is an English-based creole language with West African influences.)

It wasn't until the movie How Stella Got Her Groove Back in the 90's, which was depicted from the book by Terry McMillian that being from Jamaica finally became cool. This is when dancehall singers like Patra, Shabba, and Spragga Benz became popular. Now all my friends and American born cousins, were asking me to teach them how to dance like that.

Then in 1997, when my all-time favorite independent Jamaican film Dancehall Queen came out, my love and respect for my country grew even more. This movie told a story of a struggling single mother, who worked as a street vendor while trying to raise her two daughters. She had a man that offered her household money, in exchange he wanted her teenage daughter, a neighborhood thug that was after her brother, and the most important issue, her lack of money.

This is when she decided to take matters into her own hands and create this dancing celebrity that competed for cash prizes and became the dance hall queen. This movie made me become fascinated with the story of real dance hall queens, and I began researching them. I never knew that 15 years later, I would be writing a story inspired by them and their everyday struggles and journeys.

So, in 2013 I began writing my story of the dance hall queen but kept getting stuck. It didn't seem authentic to me. Yes, I was born on this island, but I was raised in America. So, I changed the story up some. I decided to write the story from the perception of my oldest daughter Destani's biggest fear. That one-day immigration was going to snatch me up and deport me back to Jamaica. Even adding that element to the story, it still felt like it was missing something, so again, I put the book to the side.

It wasn't until July of 2013 when I heard the story of Dwayne Jones, a homeless transgender 16-year-old boy that was murdered on the streets of Montego Bay during an Anti-LGBT attack. Not only was this child murdered, for wearing female clothing, but he beaten, stabbed, shot, and run over by a car. When I heard of this story, I was not only horrified, because this baby was the same age as my child, but it baffled me that no one was charged for his arrest because Jamaica is one of the 70 out of 195 countries in the world that still honors the buggery law. This law, also known as the sodomy law which outlaws "unnatural" and immoral sex which includes anal, oral, and bestiality.

So, I added this component in the book as well. Now that I told you where I came up with the concept of this book, I want you to understand one thing. Yes, there are many social issues in this book from deportation, LGBT, and being a dancehall queen, but the main objective that I want you as the reader to get from this book is to not judge. You may not agree with one's lifestyle, their background, their belief system, or who they want to be intimate with, but it is not for you to agree. If we all agreed on everything, we would not be human species that God put us on this earth to be. So, with that being said, I hope that you enjoy this book. After all the time that I have spent on it, I can honestly say, it has grown to be one of the best books that I have written. Sit back and enjoy!

Dedication

I dedicate this book to my best/childhood friend Steevie Washington. Baby, you are more like my brother, and I want to thank you from the bottom of my heart for loving me and my culture.
I dedicate this book to my family, but most of all, my late sister, Janet Smith. Thank you for making sure I knew where I came from.
I also dedicate this book to all the Dancehall Queens across the world. Your beauty is undeniable, and the story that you tell with your hips is beautiful.
I dedicate this book to all the West Indian people living in the United States. Make sure that your children embrace the culture that we were blessed to be products of.
Last but not least, I dedicate this book to the Gully Queens. It is hard to stay true to what you believe.

Pum Pum

John 1:3

"All things were made by Him; and without Him was not anything made that was made."

Prologue

Phe Phe

Loosening the clenching grip, I had on Iyana's hand; a feeling of peace came over me. This was the first time that I shared my story and had an opportunity to show someone that generally loves me how I used to live. It was rush hour in New Kingston, and the traffic on Trafalgar Road was at a standstill.

Weaving our way through the vehicles, I was so busy trying to ensure that we were good that I didn't notice the three youths watching us and approaching us from the opposite direction.

We were almost on the other side of the street when the group finally caught up with us. The smile that was planted on my face quickly dissipated when I noticed that they were not trying to get around us, they wanted us. Well, not us. It was me who they wanted.

It didn't take me long to recognize the youth that stood directly before me. I had seen his face many times in the photos that used to decorate my home back in D.C. It was David, Jason's son.

We stood there for what felt like an eternity and stared each other down. The pace of my heart sped up tremendously, but I was not going to let them know that they put any fear into my heart.

Slightly turning my head, I looked at Iyana and mouthed the words, "I love you," but quickly turned back to face my aggressor.

"Mi did a luk Fi yuh an kno seh mi wud a fine yuh round yah suh. Wi fine yuh. Now wi a guh kill yuh!"

Grabbing me by my hair, Jason punched me in my face over and over again. I pushed Iyana away, screaming at her, "Iyana, run! Gyal run an nuh luk back!"

Attempting to swing back didn't make any sense because his goon squad quickly grabbed each of my arms as he continued to hit me. A crowd began to form around us as they screamed out and called me all kinds of names.

The man holding my left arm pulled out a knife and handed it to David. All the fight I had in my body was gradually going away as I watched the knife coming closer to my throat. He leaned in so close to me that I was able to inhale the sour scent of the rum he had consumed earlier.

The last thing I remembered was hearing him whisper into my ear, "Now yuh a guh ded."

All of a sudden, everything went black around me as I felt him quickly pierced my throat.

August 1, 2013

Welcome to Jamaica
Iyana

"We are now about to begin our descend to Kingston, Jamaica. The local time is 2:06 pm. The weather is 86 degrees, and the sky is clear. To all of you that are here for a visit, I know that you are going to have a wonderful time, for everyone that consider Jamaica home, Welcome Home!"

The captain's voice was jovial and light as he welcomed us home to what some may consider paradise. I tried to open the window shade, but my shackled hands would not allow me to do so. The officer sitting next to noticed my struggle, reaching over me and pushed the shade open.

I was not prepared for the light that beamed onto my face, instantly warming my skin. There was not a cloud in sight allowing me to see the clarity of the ocean. Growing up in Florida allowed me to be familiar with the ocean, but I was not prepared for how clean and clear this body of water appeared. It has been almost two months since I see any body of water being housed at a family residential detention center in New Mexico.

I had to wait for the powers to be in Jamaica to approve my return. I left the island when I was only three months old and have not been back once since. Bradley promised me that once I graduated from college, we were going to take a vacation here, but now none of that mattered. I was being forced back to an island that I knew nothing about, a culture that was far from familiar to me.

"Are you excited to be back home Ms. Campbell?" Officer Davis asked me. Unlike my original thoughts of him when I first met him this morning, he was a nice man. It was not his fault that my life was turned upside down, he was just doing his job.

I shook my head, continuing to stare out the window. I refused to let him, or anyone who saw me shed a tear. I promised myself that I was going to stay strong. My parents were very vague when they spoke about Jamaica, so I knew very little about this place that I now was going to have to call my home.

It seemed like the plane was going to land in the water, but instead it touched down onto land. I closed my eyes and said a prayer under my breath, *"Dear Lord, please help me. Please protect me and help me get back home."*

I opened my eyes and waited for the plane to come to a complete stop. I took a couple of deep breaths and waited for Officer Davis to guide me off the plane and into my new reality.

Once I stepped off the plane life as I knew it changed drastically before my eyes, and I had no control of it. Officer Davis led me off the plane and to the customs department. All eyes were on me as people shook their heads and stared at me as I took my walk of shame in hand cuffs, humiliated. The video that my counselor showed me inside the detention center prepared me for this, but everything still felt unreal to me as I bowed my head and continued my trek.

According to the videos I watched, there were hundreds of deportees that arrive back at Jamaican society every week, so the people inside the airport were already looking down at me. It wasn't until I was inside the customs office that Officer Davis removed the handcuffs and sat down beside me.

"Ms. Campbell, this is the end of our journey together. The folks here will take great care of you. Don't you worry."

Even though he tried to flash me a sheepish grin, his eyes told another story. He described to me taking this flight across international lines at least 5 times a week, he has grown numb to the stories that he heard from the deportees about their unfair treatment and proclamation of innocence; I was different for him.

He had a copy of my arrest record, including my Florida id, social security card, and green card, so he was already familiar with my case. So, when he turned to me during our flight and asked me the inevitable, "What happened?" My heart sank.

Dreams

Iyana

In all honestly, I didn't know what happened my damn self. One day, I was enrolled in college with a perfect man, house, and dog; and the next, I was being arrested for possession of cocaine with an attempt to sell.

Even though I didn't know this man from Adam, I felt like it was okay to tell him my story. At first, I tried to explain to anyone that would listen to my unfortunate circumstances, but my cries fell upon deaf ears. Every one of the inmates inside the jail and the detention center had a sad story of innocence, so no one cared to hear about mine.

I stared at Officer Davis for a long time before I finally sucked in a deep breath and poured my heart out to him. I explained to him that I left Jamaica as a baby. As a matter of fact, according to my visa, it states I was three months old. I did not know anything about the island. I don't know exactly what triggered my parents to migrate to the United States, but I did know one thing. Once we touched down in Destin, Florida, we never stepped foot back onto the island.

My mother stayed at home caring for me, while my father obtained his law degree while working at the bank, and became one of the partners of Hinkle, Myers, and Campbell. He worked hard to ensure that we had a wonderful life which included us living in one of the best neighborhoods, and me attending Destin Christian Academy.

I was what you would call sheltered and naïve. My parents did their best to shelter me away from the outside world. They provided everything that I could want and need. I guess the fact that I knew that I was loved was part of the reason why I never questioned our family back in Jamaica. The only time I ever remotely asked a question was while I was doing a family tree project back in 6th grade, and I asked my mother for pictures and names of my grandparents and other known relatives.

She had a few black and white shots in the possession of her mother and father, but that was it. Her sister migrated to the UK when she was still in primary school with her mother, and that was the last time she saw them. She was left to live with her Aunt Marie in New Kingston. The moment she met my father, she felt like she had met her knight in shining armor. Although he was almost ten years her senior, he captured my mother's heart and convinced her to marry him.

Against her Great Aunt's approval, she left the poor neighborhood that they resided in and moved inside an exclusive hotel the Court Leigh Manor, downtown New Kingston. At the time, my father was the branch manager of Citibank and his job paid for him to live there since it was in the city and not in Ocho Rios, almost two hours away. My mother was in awe at the beauty of the cottages that became her new home. Everything was brand new and elegant. According to my mother, even the staff was beautiful, all of them speaking the Queen's English (the Queen of England), and while my father was at work, she would practice speaking like them. It wasn't long after that my mother informed my father that she was pregnant. My father worked many long hours, and by the time she was seven months pregnant, he was called into a meeting where his superiors offered him the chance to run the foreign exchange department in Florida.

Hard work did pay off, and by the time he was on his way home, not only were they going to take care of his immigration documents, but his wife and her new baby. This was our ticket to America! To an American, their travel agreement sounded pretty legit, but this is not America that we are talking about. We are talking about Jamaica. A place where it would cost a family thousands of Jamaican dollars at the time (now we are talking about hundreds of thousands) to obtain a green card for one person, not an entire family. I have heard stories about families that were split up so the mother or father would have to save and send for the rest of the family one at a time.

We had a good life in Destin, I had nothing to complain about until that terrible night that turned my life upside down. I was called into the office by my guidance counselor. The look on her face prepared me that what she had to tell me was not good, but I never thought in a million years that she was going to be the one that had to break the bad news to me that the loves of my world, my family, my rock were killed in a car crash by a drunk tourist. I was only 16 years old, and not ready to take on life all alone, but like I used to hear my mother say all the time that God makes no mistakes, but what in the world was I going to do now? How was I going to live?

The next couple of days went into a blur around me. Our maid Ms. Miracle informed me that she was not going anywhere to make sure I was going to be okay.

My father's law firm did everything in their power to honor me and provide a funeral for the stars. To this day, I do not remember anyone's faces, but I do remember all the love that was sent my way. Well maybe it wasn't love. Now that I am older and have been through all of this, I am not sure if it was love at all. Maybe it was the respect that they had for my father's money that was the reason.

At the time, I knew that we were okay, but it wasn't until the day before my parents' funeral when Mr. Hinkle and his nephew Bradley came to our home and sat me down with Mrs. Miracle is when I found out just how endowed my father really was.

"Your father was very resourceful and intelligent," Mr. Hinkle started off crossing his legs in front of him on our couch. "The day he started with our firm; he hired me to be his lawyer on the spot. Just in case something ever happened to him, he knew that you and your mother was going to be okay. That is why I wanted Bradley to shadow your father. I wanted him to implement his strategies, and integrity into his future practice of law."

I sat there listening to everything that he was saying. I was already aware of it all. My father practically provided a blueprint of what to do if anything ever happened to him. I knew about his burial policy, his life insurance policy that would pay off our house in case of death, and another policy that would provide monthly stipends to cover all the monthly expenses. I hated hearing about it, but I did know about it. My father was prepared. Now that I think back, maybe he was too prepared. Did he know that something was going to happen to him? Hmmmm, I wonder?

That is why I was kind of confused that Mr. Hinkle wanted to speak to me directly. My dad covered everything, including the fact that Ms. Miracle would continue being my caregiver until I was the legal age of 18.

"Yes sir, I am aware. May you please tell me what's going on? My heart can't take any more surprises. So please I am not trying to be rude, but may you please get to the point?"

I sat there with a blank look on my face and stared at the wall. I was not in the mood to hear how financially responsible my father was right now. I just wanted to lay across my bed and cry at how messed up this world really is taking both of my lifelines away from me.

Clearing his throat, Bradley flashed me a soft smile and interrupted Mr. Hinkle.

"Uncle, I agree. Maybe you should just get to the point of why we are here.

Even I am confused on what exactly is going on."

Bradley winked at me and gave the floor back to Mr. Hinkle.

"Well maybe, you are right Brad. I just wanted to share some kind words of her father. He was more like a brother to me— "

That is when the tears shown in his eyes. Taking in a few deep breaths, Mr. Hinkle tried to get himself together.

"Maybe this is not the right time for any of us, but I wanted to make you and Ms. Miracle aware that outside of the policies that he had set aside for such a tragic occasion, he also has two separate accounts for each of you. Ms. Miracle, for you taking on the complete responsibility of Iyana, Ian left you 100,000 dollars. And for you Iyana, he left 100,000 dollars for your college expenses. Last but not least, he has a trust fund set up for you that will continue collecting interest until you are twenty-one years old. Right now, there is 1.2 million in there."

Ms. Miracle and I couldn't do anything but stare at each other. Suddenly I felt a cold chill run up and down my back.

My college expenses are already taken care of, and I have a trust fund? I knew my father was on top of things, but wow this by passes everything. *1.2 million? Where did he get that much money from?*

"Are you cold?"

Bradley must have sensed my confusion from across the room, and in a moment, he was by my side covering my shoulders with his overcoat.

"No, no, I am fine?"

I looked up at him and couldn't stop staring. It wasn't until now that I realized how beautiful he was. He reminded me of Paul Walker, the star from the Fast and Furious movies. I didn't know exactly how old he was, but I knew that he was out of my league. He was a law student, so I needed to get myself together.

"Iyana, I lost my parents at a young age as well, that is why my uncle is so dear to me. I give you my word that if you ever need me, I am just one call away. I promise you."

I must not have been the only one in a trance, because Bradley never looked away. It wasn't until Ms. Miracle gently pulled my left arm that I even remembered that there were more than just the two of us in the room.

"I am sorry gentlemen," she said continuing to pull me away. I think that Iyana and I both need to take a moment to get our thoughts together. It has been a whirlwind of a time, and we still need to prepare for the funeral tomorrow. Iyana, go upstairs to your room honey. I am going to walk the two of them out."

I heard the words coming out of her mouth, but my body wasn't allowing me to move. I watched them exchange goodbyes and headed to the door. Once the lock on the door was secured behind them, that is when the tears of joy began to flood from her face.

I already signed the paperwork with your father and if anything happened, I was going to take care of you. You are like my Granddaughter Iyana, and I wasn't going anywhere regardless. But to know that your father left money for us to live on outside of what is already set up to handle the bills... That is nothing, but God. I knew that your parents were angels when I met their baby, but I wasn't ready for this.

Thank you, Lord Thank you, thank you, thank you!"

Ms. Miracle continued to rejoice as she embraced me in her arms.

"I love you, little girl. Do you know that?"

I shook my head yes and hugged her back. Just like she said, she was just like family, and now, she was all I had.

"Baby, I need you to promise me one thing," she said. "Be careful of that young man baby. I know that he means well, but my spirit just do not take to him."

I nodded my head again and walked up the stairs. Even though he left, my heart was still skipping beats. I was going to do everything in my power to let go of the thought of Bradley, but at that moment, I wasn't ready too. I was going to use my newfound thoughts of him to hopefully help the pain in my heart to go away.

Six Years Later

Perfect Record...
Gone
Iyana

"I need your license, insurance, and registration, sir," the police officer asked Bradley.

We were on our way home after a cocktail party for the firm. I was so tired that I dozed off as soon as my head touched the head rest. Bradley wanted to stay late to discuss something with his uncle, but I was ready to go many hours ago. Maxwell, my new puppy, was at home by himself, and even though we had the training pads laid out everywhere, he seemed to have separation issues and only made it to the pad if I was there with him.

I awoke by the flashlight of a police officer being shown in my face. Bradley was trying to pull his wallet out of his pocket. I waited for the officer to go back to his vehicle before I asked any questions.

"What happened, baby? Why were we pulled over? Were you speeding—"

Before I could ask any more questions, Bradley lifted his finger to lips. "I was swerving, baby," he answered. "Just a little. You know, I have this big case that I am working on, and I may have gotten too high."

High? What did he mean high? He was a practicing attorney at law! He can't choose to get high!

"Baby! What are you doing? That can affect your license!"

Bowing his head, he shook his head as I watched the tears well up in his eyes. "I know baby... I am so sorry. My uncle warned me, but I didn't listen." Suddenly, his head jerked up, and he grabbed my left hand.

"We don't have time for all of that right now," he said. "I need you to do me the biggest favor." The light from the officer's flashlight showed through the back window, startling both of us.

"Yes, baby. Whatever it is, you know I have your back. What is it?"

Taking in a deep breath, Bradley squeezed the grip that he had on my hand and whispered, "I need you to say that the drugs are yours if he makes us get out of the car. Please, baby! You do not have anything as much as a speeding ticket on your record. You have been perfect. Please, baby. Just do this for me."

Before I could respond, the officer flashed his light into both our faces. "Do you know why I pulled you over?" he asked Bradley. Even though he was talking to Bradley, he never took his eyes off of me. Something about the way he was staring at me made my skin crawl, but I had to be strong for Brad.

"Umm, yes, officer. We had a little celebration for my law firm, and I am past tired. I may have been swerving, just a little. I didn't want to wake my princess."

He flashed the officer one of his award-winning smiles, but the look on his face didn't change.

"You were doing more than just swerving. I clocked you at 98 miles per hour, while you were swerving in and out of lanes. You almost hit two vehicles! I need you to step out of the car, both of you."

Before he could respond, Bradley lifted up, unlocked the doors, and opened the driver's side door. Struggling, he attempted to stand up, but his legs were weak. If he didn't have the grip on the car door, he would have surly hit the pavement!

I watched in disbelief as I got out of the car myself. I felt like I was in the middle of a bad dream. Not only did Brad just disclose to me that he was high, but he needed me to tell the police that the drugs were mine!

I didn't even know where the drugs were at. We were driving my Range Rover, but I didn't see him place any drugs anywhere... *Unless he did it when I was asleep?*

Bradley attempted to take the sobriety test, but how pitiful he was. It showed that he was past the legal limit of anything! It didn't matter what it was!

"How much liquor did you drink, sir?" the second policeman asked as his partner guided Bradley to sit down on the sidewalk.

"I think I had maybe a glass or two," Bradley managed, "but I think it's the heroine that I snorted got me feeling like this. My girlfriend gave me a hit of hers, so that I can get home. I think I put it inside the middle console if you want to see exactly how much I took."

"What the hell!"

Were we on world's dumbest criminals? I mean, I never been pulled over by the police before, but I have watched enough television to know that you do not guide the police to the drugs! Hell! He was a lawyer! Until your legal representative comes around, you do not say anything. My father taught me that one. Damn! I wish my Daddy was here.

After that confession, it didn't take them long to have us both in the back of their police car, and my truck towed. The bumbling fool that Bradley was outside the car disappeared once we were shackled to the back of the vehicle.

"You did good, baby," he whispered to me. "Once we get to the jail, I'll call Uncle, and he will come and get us."

A good job! What the hell was he talking about? He told the police that the drugs were mine before I could and even pointed out where the stuff was.

I didn't have anything to say. I turned my head and stared out the window. If my father was alive, he would kill me! When the police asked me where I got the drugs from, I wasn't lying when I told them that I didn't know.

Once inside the station, they separated us from each other. They continued to keep me handcuffed and sat me down on a bench.

"Remove your shoes, please, and place them inside this bag," the female officer directed. She was holding open a see-through bag for me. Slowly, I removed my shows and placed them inside the bag.

Did she want me to just walk on this dirty ground without any shoes or socks?

I was smart to keep all questions that I had to myself and just waited patiently for my next step of directions. As if they could read my mind, another guard handed me a pair of orange slippers and instructed me to follow her to a desk.

Once seated, she pulled out a stack of forms from the desk drawer and started asking me a bunch of basic questions, such as name, birth date, phone number, marital status, etc.

Obediently, I answered all her questions, never pausing. I had heard so many stories from Bradley about how when some of his clients were insubordinate and disruptive after being arrested, the police actually hog tied a couple of them and obtained new charges.

"Do you know and understand the crime that you are being charged with today?" one of the officers asked. I nodded my head slowly, yes. I was sitting on the other side of the desk and let out a deep sigh o. I had never been in that kind of situation before, and I really didn't exactly know how I was supposed to respond.

Keeping up with this charade, that I am a drug user, didn't sit well with me and was very difficult for me to pretend.

"Where did you get your supply from? This is a rare stream of heroine that just hit the streets, and only the best of the best can obtain it?"

I continued to sit there in silence. Why did they keep asking me the same damn question? I already told the arresting officers that I didn't know! The officer shook her head at me and continued her interrogation of me.

"Name of your emergency contact?"

"Bradley Hinkle," I replied matter-of-factly. He was more than my emergency contact; he was all that I had.

Ms. Miracle died unexpectedly in her sleep a couple of months after I graduated from high school. Her death hurt me just as bad as the death of my parents, but Bradley was there to pick up the pieces. He held me down for so long that I was kind of obligated to be there for him in his time of need.

"Hinkle, did you say?" a male voice behind me questioned. "I heard of a Bradley Hinkle before. He's a law student, right?"

Before I could respond, another officer came over and whisked me away to get my fingerprints and mug shot. I could see the two of them still in conversation while I was on the other side of the room, but of course, I didn't know what they were saying. Something about him seemed familiar, but I could not place him.

Once I was finished processing into the jail, the officer led me to a cell, unlocked it, and nodded for me to go inside. By this time, my body was shaking uncontrollably. I didn't know what to do. My perfect record had been tainted right before my eyes, and I was going to spend the night in jail.

Reluctantly, I entered the cell and sat down on the floor closest to the door. Glancing around the room, to my surprise, there wasn't anyone else there, but I refused to make myself comfortable. The room was bare, besides a few benches and the payphone that was missing the earpiece.

"So, what's next?" I whispered to myself. They hadn't taken my clothes off of me yet, so I guess that was a good thing.

"Iyana Campbell! You are free to go!" It was the same officer that just escorted me into the cell and was now unlocking the door to let me go.

"I was bailed out?" I asked her.

The guard found my question amusing and began to laugh. "Not that quick. It takes a few hours for your information to be updated to our system. Evidently, you know some very important people that made a few late-night calls to some judges on your behalf. So, feel lucky and blessed. This doesn't happen for everyone."

I stood there in disbelief, and my body began to shake. I didn't know what to say, how to feel, or what to do. Just like that, my nightmare was over.

"Come on, girl, now! I do not have all day! Do you want to stay here? I can let them know that you like being here."

The guard grabbed my arm and damn near had to drag me out the cell. I still could not make my body cooperate. My perfect record was stolen for me just like that. I was just happy to be going home.

You are Different.

Phe Phe

"Jason!" I screamed out, gasping for air. I sat straight up in the bed while beads of sweat formed at my hairline. I could hear my heartbeat pounding in my chest as I looked around, trying to make sure that I was just having another nightmare.

It always takes me a few moments to realize exactly where I was and what was going on. I have been having the same nightmare every night since his death. Now that I am back in Jamaica, I have been living in constant fear because I trusted Jason. I am still confused on why it was a big deal for him to marry me if he was going to disrespect me the way he did.

Struggling to get out of bed, I walked over to the bathroom and stared at myself in the mirror. My eyes were bloodshot, and my skin was so damn pale. If it wasn't for the dark bags that stood out under my eyes, I would be as white as Casper, the friendly ghost.

Usually, I was so proud of my smooth, cream-colored complexion and Coolie features, but right now, after staring at myself in the mirror, I couldn't locate any beauty within my face.

Instead, I saw a sad, tired woman that could barely hold anything down. The woman's reflection that I continued to look at appeared to be one of a stranger, someone that I had never seen before.

How was it that I had allowed this man to get me to this point? Why did I allow myself to get into such a predicament?

I continued to stare at my reflection, trying to find a glimpse of me. This last week had been very hard for me. A common viral infection turned into full-blown pneumonia, forcing me to lose at least ten pounds in all of the wrong places. My hair was lifeless, and my eyes were tired. I needed some rejuvenation. I needed to get back into the swing of things and quickly.

My nightmare made me relive the harsh reality that I wanted Jason to hurt just as much as I have. I wanted him to experience the devastation of knowing that his vows had been broken by the person to whom you had dedicated your entire life.

I had done everything in my power to try and maintain our relationship, feeling completely obligated to him since he spent so much money on me, making my dream come true.

At first, I really thought I was being selfish because I used to beg my husband to stay home with me and not be out in the streets so much. I knew that he was a businessman, but he didn't have to be away from home so much when he was in town. He didn't want me to work or go to school. He wanted me to be a trophy wife for him, someone to make all his friends and colleagues jealous.

I was always accommodating and did everything in my power to make him happy. My mother used to tell my sisters and I all the time that if I wanted a happy life, I needed to be a happy wife, making sure that my husband didn't have any reason to leave home.

I think what hurt me the worst is that Jason knew all my secrets and indiscretions, but he still hurt me.

You see, I was really born a man. My name was Felix Godfrey. I have been gay my entire life, and my mother never shunned me for it. She just explained to me that being different was against the law around here, and I had to keep all my feelings to myself.

I was always told that I was a pretty boy. Both my parents were of East Indian descent, so my eyelashes are long, and my hair is shiny, straight, and black. My father was killed when I was small, leaving my mother alone in the world to care for five children all the while working as a seamstress.

Throughout my childhood, my mother worked while my siblings and I stayed home and ensured that all chores, including dinner, were complete by the time our mother made it back home. That is how I learned how to cook and clean so well. My mother always treated me like one of the girls and made sure that I was able to take care of myself one day.

It wasn't until I was about seventeen that I really understood what my mother meant by telling me to keep my feelings to myself. That was the first time a man tried to hit on me, but it wouldn't be the last.

I was walking home from school with my sisters, and men started whistling at us. I pushed my sisters along to hurry up. I did not need any drunken Rasta trying to get fresh with them, but it wasn't the girls that he wanted— it was me.

He ran up behind me and grabbed me by the hair.

"Yuh a batty bwoy?" he asked me, pulling me closer.

I stood there in fear, not knowing what to do. Even though I was a boy, one would probably describe me as being frail and dainty. I was only 5'5 and 130 pounds wet. It didn't help that I also had very small hands and feet. I was not created to be a protector, but because of my size, my mother made sure I knew how to be a fighter.

"Lemme go," I said to him, trying to free myself from his grip.

"Answer me nuh. Are yuh a batty bwoy? Do yuh wan to suk mi dick?" He licked his lips, waiting for me to respond.

I responded all right, punching him straight in his stomach, taking all of the wind away from him. Bending over in pain, he let me go. My sisters and I ran the rest of the way home, waiting for our mother to return.

As soon as she entered, my baby sister, Lisa, told her what happened. She listened to everything, then told the girls to go to their room.

"Come here, Felix. Tell me, what did he say to you?"

Embarrassed, I lowered my head and repeated the horrible words that he said to me in barely a whisper.

She looked around, making sure the girls were not anywhere around and asked me if I knew what that meant. I nodded my head, yes, still keeping my head down low.

"In Jamaica, there is a law called the Buggery Law that makes it illegal for a man to have sex with another man. You know that, right?" she asked me, holding my arm. "Felix, have you ever had sex before?"

I shook my head no, eyes still on the ground.

"Look at me, bwoy, and answer me again. Have you ever had sex before?"

"No, Mummy," I replied, tears filling up my eyes.

She stared at me a few more moments, and then finally, gave me a hug.

"Felix, you must not let anyone know what is going on inside your head, okay. I don't know what I would do if I lost you."

I promised my mother that I would be careful, and it wasn't me that let the cat out of the bag. It was my second eldest sister, Janine, who was always jealous of the bond I had with my mother. During my graduation dinner, my life changed right before my eyes.

After we finished saying grace, she politely said, "Mummy, Felix was in your makeup again, calling himself 'Phe Phe.' Uncle David, isn't there something wrong with a man that wants to be a woman?"

An occasion that was meant to be celebratory became instant shunning, and my uncle demanded that I leave his brother's home immediately.

Before I knew it, he and his brothers were beating me and dragging me out of the house at the same time. They threw me out without any clothes or shoes, besides the items that I was wearing.

My mother was arguing and fighting for me, but all of that fell upon deaf ears. Even though what my uncle said was correct, it still hurt that I was the one that was going to be all alone. If the community found out, my mother's house could be burned down, and then they all would be homeless. Technically, I was a man now and needed to stand up on my own two feet.

Jason found me when I was down and out, living underground in a sewer system with a group of gay men off of Trafalgar Road. He saved me. We lived down there together because at least we could look out for one another and protect each other. Some men worked as prostitutes, while others would do petty crimes. Others, like me, would do odds and ends jobs to try to make some money. We were known to society as the "gully queens." I ended up there because just like my uncles had predicted: once people knew your secret, everyone was against you.

Gay and down-low men would frequent the gully, looking for someone to keep them warm at night. By this time, I was twenty years old and still a virgin. I had never had sex with a man or woman, but I knew that I wanted to be with a man. I also knew that I wanted my first time to be special.

When I met Jason, he and two men were down in the gully, looking for someone to for the night. At first, he thought I was a woman because I had let my hair grow out long down my back.

"You are beautiful," he told me, running his fingers through my hair. I pulled away from him, but something about him intrigued me.

"If you are looking for a whore, mi nuh da one."

I didn't care how much this man was making me blush; I was not going to sleep with him for fun or for free. He shook his head laughing loudly, and that was the spark of our conversation. He was actually there with his friend, who was too nervous to go alone. He wasn't looking for anyone that night, but when he saw me, he just knew he had to speak to me.

That was the beginning of our beautiful relationship. He moved me out of the gully and into his Kingston home. Jason worked for the embassy in D.C. and had become an American citizen. He stayed half the time in the U.S., and half the time in Jamaica. He still had children with his ex-wife and wanted to make sure he was very involved in their lives. They went to the American International School of Kingston and were very well taken care of.

When he got my green card approved to go with him to America, I was elated. I was even happier that for my twenty-first birthday, he took me to the doctor for a check-up. Well, I thought it was a check-up. It was actually an orientation for reconstructive surgery. The entire process took over two and a half years, and I owed the entire process to him.

"Baby, it is not going to be easy, but I will most definitely do everything in my caliber to make you happy and support you the entire way," he told me.

I was convinced that our life was perfect and couldn't get any better. I believed in this philosophy up until almost a year ago when I found out that I was HIV positive. That is when my nightmare began, and I went crazy on Jason. During and a little while after my surgery, I had so much blood work done that I knew I was clean up until a certain point. This told me that the disease hadn't happened from a blood transfusion or surgery. I was HIV positive because of Jason.

A year later, and I'm still tortured by dreams of him and his betrayal. I sat alone, staring into the darkness around me, trying to quiet the demons of my past.

As if someone was reading my mind, my phone began to ring. At first, I assumed that it was Mason because he was the last person I had spoken to on the phone, and I had dozed off in the process.

Uncovering my head from beneath the pillow, I patted around the bed and found my phone. I quickly glanced at the caller's I.D. before I answered, but it was a private number, so I wasn't sure who it was.

"Hello," I said.

The person on the other line was silent, and that made chills run up and down my spine. I have been living in fear since I came back from the States. I don't trust anyone. If anyone knew that I used to be a man, my life would be over. I needed to get better and quickly, so I could finally leave my house.

I hung up the phone and tried to lay back down. The eerie feeling still lurked throughout my body as I tried to clear my head.

I set an alarm for 7:30 a.m. and rolled back over, trying to find sleep once more.

4th of July

Iyana

"Right there, baby. Mmmmm, right there!" I moaned as Bradley thrust my hips down on his pelvis over and over again. It was almost noon, and we had been going at it for hours. It had been only a few weeks since I had gone to court, and everything was going well. I pleaded guilty on the advice of my now-fiancé and his uncle. They got me probation for three years.

The moment I stepped out of the jail, Bradley and his uncle were there waiting for me. "Thank you, baby! Thank you!" Bradley had cried, embracing me. "I always knew that you were brave, but this time, you went above and beyond!" In a flash, he was down on one knee, looking me straight in my eyes. "Will you marry me girl?"

I didn't know what to say. Finally, I cried tears of joy, saying how much I loved Bradley, and of course, I would marry him.

So now, here I am, making love to my soon-to-be husband when we should have been getting ready for our 4th of July celebrations.

I woke Bradley up at 8 a.m., so we could have some time to snuggle before he went out to start the grill, but Bradley had other agendas on his mind. He leaned in and kissed me, making my body quiver uncontrollably. I melted like butter. His kiss was so passionate, soft, and so slow that it didn't matter that the morning breath was lingering in the air. The way he whispered my name made my honeypot wet.

Four hours later, I was straddled on top of him, cumming again for the thousandth time, bouncing up and down, gyrating with so much force that I had to hold onto the headboard. I had a Vise-Grip lock on it for balance and support.

Even though it had been five years since this man had taken my virginity, I still had to take in deep breaths every time he penetrated me. Although Bradley is a white boy— don't believe the hype! My soon-to-be husband was well endowed, and my body still has to adjust go get used to him!

"BABY!!! I AM ABOUT TO CUM! ARE YOU READY? ARE YOU READY?!" he yelled as he thrust his hips into my body one last time. I pushed my body down with all my might, trying to ensure that I caught all his children inside of me.

"Honey, are you ready to get in the shower? We have to get dressed?" he asked. "Can you turn the shower on for me?" Playfully, Bradley pushed me off of him and headed towards the bathroom.

He can't be serious right now, I thought to myself, stretching my arms up over my head. "Okay, baby, give me a second. I need to catch my breath. This sexy ass individual came out of nowhere and screwed my brains out this morning! Give me a few," I said through a big smile.

Bradley is so damn sexy, I thought to myself, admiring the firmness of his ass, making me want him all over again. I was so happy that in a few months, I would be Mrs. Hinkle. I was so excited, but I wished my parents and Ms. Miracle could be there to celebrate with me. However, I knew in my heart that they would be with me in spirit.

Hearing the shower start, I rolled over onto my stomach and closed my eyes.

"You act like I am the baby! Part of the reason why I picked you was because you were so much younger than me. I needed someone to wear me out, not vice versa!"

Yes, I am almost nine years younger than him, but one would never know it. He had the finesse and sophistication of a man twice his age, but the face of a young boy. Bradley was not someone that came from a family that gave him handouts. He worked hard for everything he had. Yes, he ended up moving in with me into my parents' home, but he paid for the extensive remolding of the infrastructure. He knew that it was hard for me to come home to a place where I had grown up with both of my parents my entire life, so Bradley gutted it out and made it have a contemporary feel on the inside.

At first, I was horrified by the idea, but after I seen the ending results, I was glad that he did it. Even though he was a lawyer, Bradley could have been an interior designer.

I had to admit, Bradley was the complete package: sex appeal, brains, and an abundance of patience that can make you go crazy. Bradley was always a step ahead of a situation, another trait that I have grown to love.

I heard the water pressure change, which meant that Bradley was in the shower. I waited a few more moments and quietly rolled out of the bed to join him.

Quietly, I opened the curtain and laid my head against his back, wrapping my arms around his waist. Bradley turned around, facing me.

"You are so beautiful to me, little girl," he whispered into my ear before kissing me. The semi-hot water felt so good against my body and my hair. Slowly, Bradley ran his fingers up my body and towards my head. Guiding me all the way under the shower head, he gently began to wash my hair.

My blondish brown curls made me appear to be mixed. Every time an African American woman asked me what I'm mixed with, and I told them I was Jamaican, I either got one of two responses: "No wonder, you are so exotic," or my favorite one, "There are light-skinned people in Jamaica?" Either one made me uncomfortable about my skin tone and naturally curly tresses. Both of my parents were fair-skinned, so I didn't really have any rebuttal for it.

I leaned in for another kiss, ready to take on another round from my boy toy, when I heard *Ding-Dong*, the chime of the doorbell.

"Dammit, baby! Folks are already here. I told you I couldn't be fooling you! Now look, someone is already outside." Chuckling, Bradley pulled me in tighter and kissed like it was our last time. "It's probably my uncle. You know, he is a stickler for promptness."

There was another sound that came from our front door, but it wasn't the doorbell. This time it was a heavy, long knock. Someone was serious about getting in, so I pushed Bradley off of me and hurried out the shower, wrapping my robe around me.

I dried my feet off the rug and dashed down the stairs.

"Just a minute!" I yelled out, rushing to the door. I looked out of the peep hole and saw an officer on the other side of my door.

"Why in the hell is the police here?" I asked softly under my breath. Ever since my arrest ordeal, I developed a newfound phobia for them. The palms of my hands quickly became moist. I stood there, not knowing what to do. The knock started again, intensifying.

By that time, Bradley was behind me, confused about what was going on.

On every show that I have watched where the police came to your door, it usually meant bad news. No matter what it was, mentally, I was not prepared for it.

"The police are out there," I whispered to Bradley. He wrapped his arms around me, trying to calm me down.

Bradley stepped in front of me and opened the door. I didn't even realize that he had gotten dressed until I thought about it later.

"Yes?" Bradley asked the officer, pushing me behind him. There was a S.W.A.T. team of police outside my door.

"My name is Officer Hayden. I am with I.C.E, Immigration and Customs Enforcement. Can we go inside? We are here for Iyana Campbell."

For me! My heart began thumping inside my chest as I waited for the officer to respond.

"What do you want with her?" he asked, the officer never budging from his spot.

"We have a warrant for her arrest to be deported back to her country, Jamaica."

Warrant? Deportation? What the hell is going on? Again, this time, I wrapped my arms around his waist, holding on for dear life.

"Look, sir! I didn't break down your door because today is a holiday. So, we can do this the easy way or the hard way. She recently pleaded guilty for a drug charge, and we got an anonymous tip that there was a large number of the form of drugs that she got caught with."

"Hey! Look Bradley, let us in now," a familiar voice yelled out. I glanced around him, and the officer that I had seen in the jail was outside my house.

"You don't remember me, Bradley? I was the arresting officer of Sasha, your previous girlfriend. Sasha was arrested in a similar situation. Don't worry about it. I am not done. I am coming back for you."

They know each other? What the hell is going on? Who is Sasha?

Bradley's body began to shake. "I-I-I don't know who you are," he said. "I am Iyana's lawyer, and I need to see your warrant."

I heard paper shuffling. It felt like an eternity before he put the documents in Brad's hands.

"Wow, you do have a warrant. I-I-I don't know what to say."

It was already embarrassing knowing that the police and I.C.E. officials were outside my parents' home with a warrant for me; I didn't want any of our friends or family to see me being arrested again.

"I am Iyana Campbell. I am not a drug dealer. I didn't do anything wrong."

Before I knew it, the officers pushed past Bradley and grabbed me. That was the last thing I remembered before I hit the floor. All of a sudden, everything went black.

F.U.R.I.
Iyana

So, that was how I ended up back in Jamaica. A country I knew very little about due to situations that were based on circumstances. Officer Davis patted my shoulder as the female customs officer came out from the back, calling my name.

"Iyana Campbell?"

The sound of her voice reminded me of the sweet way my mother used to say my name. Reluctantly, I stood up and smiled a sad good-bye to the only person that I knew.

"Hello, Ms. Campbell," she said to me as Officer Davis passed her the thick manila envelope that possessed my life story. "My name is Inspector Taylor. I will be processing your intake interview."

She stepped to the side and instructed me to go down the hallway. "My office is the first one on the left," she said. I found it easily and sat down in front of her desk, rubbing my wrist. Even though Officer Davis said that he made them as loose as he could, my wrists still ached with red marks all over them.

"Iyana, provide for me the complete spelling of your full name and your date of birth."

I recited my information for the hundredth time within the last couple of months, and I knew this wasn't my last. The questions she asked me were very few and basic, allowing the interview to be complete within ten minutes.

"Your interview was fairly easy because you came back with all your identity," she said to me while passing me a stack of papers. I was happy about how quickly the process took but was reminded that I was a convict when she removed my green card and passport from the pile. *I'm really not getting punk'd,* I though. *This shit is really serious.*

"Make sure you do not lose this form. It is form C27. It allows you to be able to ship 600 American dollars' worth of your personal property for free, but you have to have this complete within a six-month period. Do you have any bags?" I nodded my head. "Let's go to baggage claim."

I stood up as she did, and I followed her to baggage claim. It wasn't hard finding my bag because it was the last one on the belt. Hopefully, I would not need a care package sent to me of my personal belongings because I still had faith in my heart that Bradley was going to come get me. He promised me that he would, as I left my home shackled, not even afforded the opportunity to kiss him or my puppy good-bye.

In a blink of an eye, my family was pulled away from me just that quickly, and there was nothing I could do about it. I think that is what bothered me the most. The amount of control that I didn't have. I shook my head trying to get the thoughts of home out of my head. This was my home now, Jamaica, and I was not going to be able to attempt to adjust to my new lifestyle if I kept daydreaming about the past.

She led me out the door, and finally, I had the opportunity to take in Jamaica, well, at least the airport. There was a lot of bustles outside, but I have to say that Norman Manley International Airport reminded me of and, in some cases, was better than some of the airports that I flew in and out of in the States. Once outside the airport, the scenery was a tad different. I was used to a bunch of yellow cabs and mini shuttles hovering outside the doors, hoping that someone would choose their vehicle as their means of transportation, but this was different. There were a lot of little vans and cars parked outside with men and women standing in front of them, holding up signs to identify who they were. The only time I've seen anything remotely similar was when I was in New York, and there were gypsy cars (unofficial cabs) lined up like yellow cabs.

"Have you spoken to any of your family, letting them know that you are here?" she asked me while waving to a group of men and women standing in front of a white van. Their sign read: F.U.R.I. I didn't know who they were because the video I watched spoke of NODM, the

National Organization of Deported Migrants.

I shook my head, no, as we walked over to them and handed me my packet. The only person I knew as family was my great aunt, and I didn't believe that she was still alive. There was just me. I was officially alone in the world.

"It was nice meeting you, Iyana! I wish you the best of luck, and may God bless you.

"The good people from the Family Unification & Resettlement Initiative will take care of you. This organization is ran completely by deportees and will do anything in their power to make this a smooth and easy transition for you."

"Hello Miss, my name is Mary, and I am your mentor. Do you have anyone that you need to call?" she asked, handing me a phone, while the guys were putting my things in the van. I was a little nervous to leave them alone, but at this point, I didn't have an option.

A tinge of excitement exploded inside of my stomach, and my hope was reinstated. "Can I call overseas? I needed to call my fiancé at home."

"LOL, I am referring to family members here on the island. There is a lot of stuff that we have to do together at first over the next couple of days, like getting a TRN number, but after that, I promise you that I will help you find your family. Matter of fact, what is your surname?"

"Surname? What does that mean?"

"Your last name," Mary answered.

Laughing nervously, I provided all the information about my aunt that I did know. For the first time since I got on this island, I was beginning to feel a little hope, and for me, that was big. I hopped inside the van and sat down quit.

Lord, you have not forsaken me, I prayed, *ever since the ICE inspectors stole me from my home, but today, I truly do believe that now, I do have something to live for.*

Reunited and it feels.

So good.... | think.

Iyana

5:10 AM. That is what time the clock on the dresser read. It is not until the world is taken away from you that you really sit back and realize you took for granted the little things, something as small as a window to look out of. Even though I was not in jail, it still felt like it. The room that I was given was smaller than the jail cell I had lived in the United States. I was thankful that it was clean, and I was given three meals a day, but my iPhone was blank. I looked out the window, then back down at my phone. No missed calls. No texts.

"Should I call him?" I asked myself under my breath. "Is he thinking of me?"

Gripping the pre-paid cellphone with my left hand, I rubbed the beads of sweat off of my forehead with my right. It is so hot in here, and the little fan that I had on the dresser was not doing anything but blowing out hot air. I felt like a convict that was sentenced to solitaire confinement. I turned the light switch on and continued to stare at my phone.

I am thankful that Mary took me under her wing like a little sister. She had given me this pre-paid phone, the American SIM card, and a Jamaican SIM card. I had already wasted a lot of minutes calling my house in Florida and Bradley's cell phone that was ridiculous. Until I found a job, it was all I had, and with my deportee status hovering over my head, I had to make life decisions with every phone call.

I dialed three digits of his number and hung up. I knew that he was not going to answer. I couldn't believe that he wouldn't return my calls. Even though I didn't have anywhere to put my items, I still needed some things and money to get my life on track here. I tried to call his uncle as well, but no answer from him either.

I stood up and started pacing back and forth in my little dungeon. I couldn't take this too much longer. I had played enough mind games with myself to see that I was alone in the world. I have been living there for 45 days and halfway through my allotted time.

Time, money, and energy is of the essence, and I was running out of momentum. Every time I closed my eyes, I would dream about that last intimate moment that Bradley and I shared, and then how the ICE officers whisked me away and changed my life forever.

The last month and a half had been complete hell for me. I tried to keep myself motivated, reminding myself that I had control of my destiny and as long as I would fight and not break down, I could make some sort of a life.

The last six months had been hell for me. I kept hope alive up until the first day that I was denied a job due to my deportation status. I couldn't believe it. They act as if I am an ex-felon, but I guess I am to them. I had a chance to get out of Jamaica, and I had messed it up. And I guess I did. Even though I told the judge that drugs were not mine, he still signed the papers for me to be deported.

I didn't fight the judge at all. I looked back at Bradley as he said nothing at all. I think that is what hurt me the worst. The fact that he didn't take a stand and admit that the drugs were his. Fuck his law license! These people were taking me away from the only life that I knew, and this fool had nothing to say at all.

It was when I accepted that I only had this tiny area to reside in with someone else controlling when I turned on and off the lights, nothing compared to my five thousand square foot house in America, that the reality of my life as I now knew it came to me.

Not only did Bradley, but my so-called fiancé also abandon me, he had the audacity to avoid me and not even help me get my personal items. What kind of man turns his back on the woman he supposedly loves? Especially so easy and so quickly?

When I told Mary about the situation, the first thing she asked was, "Did he set you up?"

The question blew me out of the water, but hey, at this point, what else could I think?

Ms. Mary would stop by to check up on me after her shift to make sure that I was okay. We would sit and drink tea. The conversation would always come around to me getting back into school. At first, I was waiting on my TRN, Jamaican social security number, to come back, but that is when I realized I was out here alone and had to fend for myself. I needed to get a job first, but after so many attempts, school was back to being the number one option.

Ms. Mary was a deportee as well, so she had been through everything that I was going through. She had been trying to get me in to work for one of the few organizations out there to assist with aid for deportees, but since the outside job world was scarce for us, I could see why there were not any openings.

"Chile, you are losing too much weight! You need to eat! What man is going to want you all skin and bones?"

A man wanting me? That entire ordeal had made me feel unworthy of love and compassion. I had just taken a man's ring, accepting to be his wife soon, and in the blink of an eye, I was left all alone.

I had not been able to eat or sleep. I was completely aware that I had lost weight because the few items that I did have to wear were all too big for me. My once full and vibrant, curly tresses were now limp.

I had been begging Bradley on his voicemail so many times to help me or at least explain to me why he turned his back on me. Anything for an answer as to why he left, and he still wouldn't talk to me. I had sent emails and text messages, all went unanswered. Literally, I had no way to communicate with him. The only means of communication that I have had with him has been through his attorney.

I had been going out of my mind trying to figure out what happened to make him turn his back on me like that. I could see the rest of the world doing so because they did not know why I did what I did, but not him. Now, I was in Jamaica, not able to concentrate on what I needed to do next because I couldn't get this asshole out of my head.

Sprawled across the bed, I fought to get comfortable. *Dammit! I need some cool fucking air!* I dropped my phone on the ground and curled up in a ball. I was not going to call him again. *Well, at least not tonight.*

I closed my eyes as the tears flowed from my eyes. I could not keep feeling this way. I had to start thinking with my head because allowing my heart to lead was what got me into this situation.

I had dreams of becoming Mrs. Bradley Hinkle. I needed to feel his touch on the small of my back. He was my savior, my rock, and I never questioned his judgment. He rescued me when I had nothing else in the world. I let him control me and my life out of the palm of his hands.

We used to joke on so many occasions for him to make sure and not break my heart. I gave Bradley control of everything, including my parents' money, and this was the thanks that I got to show for it?

Out of nowhere, my phone rang, startling me. My phone never rung, especially not at this time of the morning, so I was afraid to answer it.

"Hello?" I barely whispered into the phone.

Could Bradley feel my sense of urgency that I needed him right now? Was he missing me like I was missing him?

"Iyana is that you?" the soft, raspy female voice questioned me through the phone.

Releasing the breath that I was holding; I was trying to figure out who it was on my other line.

"Yes, this is Iyana, who am I speaking with?"

"Oh! Praise Jesus! Jesus! Jesus! This is your Aunt Madge! Madge Taylor! Your mother left me and went to the States with your father. Please come home. You are welcome to have her room. Please baby, come on home."

Tears sprung from my eyes as I listened to her talk to me. *I do have a family. I do have someone that wants me.* I couldn't wait to thank Mary. She promised me that she was going to find my family, and she did.

We made arrangements for me to come by tomorrow to see her. By the time I hung up the phone, an air of peace rained down on me. It was going to be the first time in a long time that I was able to go to sleep.

Welcome to the Garrisons

Iyana

I took the bus and rode it to the area my Great Aunt called Tivoli Garden. I followed Mary's precise directions all the way to her front door. As I walked through the neighborhood, I didn't know how to feel about it. The building reminded me of the ones located in the French Quarter of New Orleans, after Hurricane Katrina.

The buildings were painted pastel colors, but there were traces of devastation throughout the entire area. At first, I thought it was because the neighborhood was located so close to the ocean side, but it didn't take long to see that some sort of a war had taken place here.

There were so many little children playing in the street that I didn't want to believe that something like that could have happened, but the infrastructure told its own story.

I felt like a little kid on the way to the candy store. I am glad I had the chance to live in the halfway house first before I met my aunt, or I would not have it in me to appreciate the little things.

I walked up to the front door and paused. I didn't know what to say to her exactly. I wanted some sort of sense of normalcy. I wanted to feel like I belonged. Mary was supposed to meet me over here after she got off work. She found my aunt because she is the neighborhood baker, Ms. Taylor.

Every Saturday, she made little treats from scratch, porridge, bread, and rice pudding. She had been feeding the children for years, so everyone in the area had heard of her. Mary thought there was a possibility that she was my aunt, but never got a chance to ask her because she was in the hospital for some time battling pneumonia. She was discharged on Friday and was back to baking on Saturday. That was when she had the opportunity to ask her.

As soon as she told my aunt about my father and mother's name, she knew exactly who I was. Now, I was about to meet a woman that my parents ran across the ocean to get away from. Hopefully, she welcomes me with open arms. If not, it was back to the shelter for me.

I knocked on the door and waited a few moments for her to answer. All eyes were on me as people passed. It was completely obvious that I was not from around there. A couple of teen boys even whistled at me as they rode past on their bikes.

"Iyana!" a beautiful woman with the shiniest gray hair, neatly pulled back into a bun, quickly wrapped her arms around me.

"You look just like your mother! You are so pretty. It don't matter the reason why you are here, but I do know God makes no mistakes. You are home, baby. Finally, you are home!"

I followed my aunt into her small, but neat home. She had pictures all over the walls, some even of me. She had every school picture that I have taken from kindergarten all the way up to the 10th grade. That is when I put two and two together. My mother had been updating her of me from afar.

What was the real reason why my mother kept me away from her then? Not today, but at some point, after we get better acquainted, I was going to ask her to tell me her side of the story.

At eighty-three years old, she was walking around, singing and dancing like a teenager while she set my plate at the table. It was full of cantaloupe, rice, peas, and stewed chicken. There was a bowl in the middle of the table filled with fresh peppers.

At first, I declined, but Aunt Madge was not taking no for an answer. So, I sat down and bowed my head as she poured me some water. The aroma from the table smelled so good, but I was not ready for how good the first bite was going to be.

It didn't take me long to get lost in my plate, eating in complete silence. When I took the last bite, she finally took in a deep breath and asked me the inevitable, "Do you need some money?"

I didn't say anything as I stared at my plate. I could not take any money from her. If she was in communication with my mother, then she must have known that we were doing well. To take from her now would be terrible.

"No ma'am. I am okay."

I couldn't bear to look her in the face. She just met me for the first time today, and she wanted to help me out financially already.

My aunt grabbed my chin and made me look her in the eyes. "I know that man has control of your money in the States," she said, "and has not sent you anything. Do not be proud, baby. That is what family is for. I will help you." She kissed my forehead and ran back into the kitchen.

Two Months Later

University of West Indies
Iyana

I finally got my ducks in a row and was ready to register for school. I moved all the weigh in with my aunt, and even though I slept on the couch, and we lived in fairly poor conditions, she did everything in her power to make me comfortable, and that was all that mattered.

There was a flag on my TRN, so that is why it took a little longer for me to utilize it. Now that everything was clear, I was up bright and early, trying to get into school. There was still no word from Bradley, and I still only had the few items I was able to bring with me on the plane.

I did my best to be like the fashionistas I used to watch on TV and change my pieces up at first, but now I didn't care. I was embarrassed every time my aunt asked me to have, I heard from him. I ran out of excuses and didn't know what else to tell her. So, I stopped answering— well, at least verbally. Now every time she asked the same question, I just nodded my head. I needed to do something good to get both of our minds off of the fact that this man was living in my big house, while my aunt and I lived in a one-bedroom apartment.

When I arrived at the University, I was floored at how beautiful it was. Considering the fact that I was living in what we would call in the States a "project apartment," that the electricity sometimes was turned off due to the government rationing it, this place was like a palace to me. Everyone was friendly, and the aroma of intelligence stood out in the air.

I asked a group of girls where the registrar's office was located. I was going to be a new student! I had my packet of personal items. I just got my official transcript from both the high school and college that I attended back home. I went to the FURI office and used the computer that they had for public use.

I knew that I was a little late to apply to be a new student and passed the deadline for entrance, but I figured if I came down and told them my story in-person, they would feel sorry for me.

Once inside the registrar's office, I went on the computer and registered for admission. It told me to give it 2-4 days for processing. I figured that it wouldn't hurt to get everything together for financial aid. This is when my deportation affected me again.

I stood in line and looked around the room. There were only a handful of people in the office, so it wasn't hard to notice the pretty girl reading alone in the big chairs as her head kept bouncing to a beat.

She had the richest almond skin complexion and straightest black hair. She reminded me of a mix between a Native American woman that lived on a reservation and a black woman. I couldn't help but stare at her. Her attire was very basic, but chic. I was so engulfed with her that I didn't pay attention to the gentleman behind the counter, calling out next.

"Hello, my name is Iyana Campbell, and I am a transfer student from the US. I would like to apply for any scholarships, loans, and grants that you may have available."

"What program do you want to enroll into?"

"Education," I responded.

After a few more moments, he looked up and said, "Sorry Miss, there are no cash bursars available for your degree study."

I paused for a moment. "Okay. "How do I apply for loans?"

"Miss, the only loans we have are short-term loans, and they are only given to people that have confirmed money coming in. In your circumstance, we do not have anything for you."

The old me would have had a full-fledged debate on the subject, but at this moment, I was over it. I had no more fights in me. I didn't say anything else to the man. I looked around and had to quickly find a seat. I needed to get my thoughts together, though I felt like I couldn't breathe.

I couldn't fight anymore; I couldn't pretend like everything was going to be okay. *How was I going to get into school if I couldn't afford it?* The tears that fell from my eyes could lay a ton of bricks. I couldn't pretend anymore. All my fears had come to life, and I couldn't hold back anymore.

I didn't care anymore about who was going to see me like this. I just needed to get this out. I was so lost in my cry that I didn't sense the pretty, exotic-looking girl standing over me.

"Are you okay?" she asked, rubbing my head. It took me a moment to respond, but I finally shook my head, no. The only people that knew about my issues with ICE were the people involved, my aunt, and my friend, Mary.

"My name is Phoebe, but you can call me Phe-Phe. Tell me what happened, literally, I got all day."

Money Makes the World Go Around

Iyana

Like a lost puppy, I followed "Phe-Phe" to another sitting area in the lobby that was quiet. I couldn't help admiring her as she walked. The way she swayed, the fullness of her hips was beautiful and rhythmic. Something about her stood out, made you notice her. I don't know why someone like her would care about what was wrong with someone like me, but I was just happy that I had anyone that wanted to hear what was wrong.

As I sat across from her, I hesitated before I spoke. Blowing out a deep breath,

I meekly said, "Hello, my name is Iyana, and I am an American deportee."

I felt like I was in an Alcoholics Anonymous meeting, but just saying that little bit made me feel that much better.

I waited to see her response after I told her the truth. So many people had scolded me, or they simply got up and walked away, assuming I must have been a drug dealer that got caught. Technically, that was what my papers read, but I knew my truths.

Phe Phe removed the sunglasses she was wearing and looked me directly in the eyes. "I am a deportee too," she said. "From the United States as well. I actually lived in D.C."

I sat straight up in my seat and shook my head. *She was a deportee as well? She didn't look common or as if she was struggling. How was she making it?*

"I know, I know, I got a lot of my stuff sent over, including some money I had saved. That is how I was able to survive. Let me guess, your family in America turned their back on you once you arrived? So many people share that story with you. All you have to do is get over your pity party, and make it do what it do. That is my advice to you.

"So, you were in school over there? How far along were you? I couldn't help but hear you tell the clerk that you were a transfer student. This is not like America where you can just go in and apply for Pell Grants and loans. What a lot of people have to learn once they arrive back in Jamaica is that this is not the States. There is no welfare system, housing authorities, WIC offices that can just subsidize your means of life.

"When you are poor in Jamaica, you are just poor. I moved to America four years ago, so when I arrived and saw all the resources that were there, it encouraged me that I was not going to be poor anymore. And I stayed true to myself even after deportation."

I took in everything that she was saying and reflected on it for a moment. Here, she was a true Jamaican that went over to America, tried to make a living for herself, got deported, came back to Jamaica, and was still determined to do better.

I told her my story blow-by-blow, piece by piece. Phe-Phe never responded, just gave me her undivided attention. When I finished laying out all my dirty laundry, she stood up and did something that I totally was not expecting. She pulled me up to a standing position, giving me a firm hug. Tears were in her eyes, so I knew something that I had said affected her. I just did not know which part. Moments later, she released our embrace and held both of my hands.

"I am a victim as well of a man taking advantage of my heart, my weakness. I have an immigration lawyer that has been diligently working on overturning my deportation. I know if he can fix my case, he can really clear your name altogether."

She continued to hold my hands while choking up on her own tears.

"Iyana, you are beautiful, and people sometimes takes advantage of you, especially when you are vulnerable. I am going to give you a present. I will pay for your first class here, just to get you back into the swing of things, but I am also going to teach you how to take care of yourself.

Once you get back on track, thank me by paying for one of my classes."

I stared at her in disbelief. *She has enough money to cover my tuition.* One US dollar equals 117 Jamaican dollars, so it sounds awkward to hear that she was going to cover a class that cost 105,396.61 Jamaican dollars.

The only job that I could think of that could produce a large sum of money like that was prostitution, and I was definitely no whore. Before I agreed to that, I had to make it clear that I was not going to sell my ass for anything. When I told her my fears, Phe-Phe just laughed at me.

"I would never put another woman out on the track to work," Phe-Phe said, "but I am going to teach you how to use your body to get what you want. Do you have plans tonight? Meet me out tonight." She wrote the address down on a piece of paper, and then went over to the bursar's office. She spoke to the clerk that I spoke to and pointed over to me.

After a few more minutes, she pulled out some money from her purse and handed it to him. He printed something out and handed it to her.

She waved me over, motioning for me to hurry up. Walking briskly, I approached the desk, trying to get my emotions together. Everything was going so quickly that it took my mind a second to comprehend it all.

"Okay, Miss. Here is your receipt for your payment. I made you a mock registration since you were not in the system yet, and now, you have a credit on your account. You can go ahead and pick your class now or do it online. I hope you ladies have a good day."

Phe-Phe flashed him a huge smile and guided me out the door. I bit my lip, so that I would keep the tears from flowing. *God blesses the faithful.* That is what my aunt told me every day before I walked out her door. Today was the first time that I started to believe what she said.

Once outside the school, Phe-Phe gave me another big hug.

"Make sure you meet me tonight. I have some stuff to take care of now, but I promise you, I will help you get back on track in no time."

I stood there still at a loss for words as she walked away. Whatever she wanted me to do, I would at least give it a try. Anything was better than what I had going on now. I looked up to the heavens and mouthed, "Thank you, God," several times before walking out to the main street to catch a bus home.

Club Quad

Iyana

Stepping out of the cab, I wasn't sure how I felt about the atmosphere that was taking place around me. Quad Night Club was bumping, and my nervousness was gradually going away. The bass was beating through the speakers, and a singer was crooning, *Popcorn is the only man she wants... Only man she wants...*

The vibe was nothing like I had ever seen before. It was totally different from the United States. The girls were dressed very provocatively, almost naked, and it didn't seem strange to anyone. I thought the sundress that I picked out was cute and would allow me to fit in for sure, but I was totally wrong. I was overdressed compared to the rest of the women around me, literally.

The colorful wigs and bright articles of clothing had me mesmerized, watching the girls sway past me.

"Yuh a gwan guh inside or stand here, and watch?"

I turned around smiling from ear to ear as Phe-Phe leaned in and hugged me tight. She was just as beautiful as the other women here, wearing a bright green body suit that cupped her in all the right places.

I followed Phe-Phe as she walked right up to the door and did not have to wait in any lines to go through the door.

"Wuh Gwan Gyal?" the man at the door asked her, smiling a big toothless grin.

"Dis mi friend, make sure she get a VIP band now!"

The man looked me up and down, shaking his head. The look on his face made it clear that he did not approve of my clothing, but that didn't stop him from putting the band around my left hand and waved us inside.

Damn, I'm spoiled! I thought to myself as we walked into the club. I was used to being ushered to the VIP section by the hostess. This club was totally different from what I was used too. There were fluorescent lights flashing all over the place and photographers were snapping pictures everywhere.

The club reeked of cigarettes and weed. Everyone seemed to know Phe-Phe, treating her as if she were royalty. My eyes scanned the area for an empty seat, but I did not locate one. The place was jammed packed, and everyone was having such a great time. Everyone that is, but me.

A heavy-set man was waving to me to meet him at the bar. At first, I wasn't sure exactly who he was waving at, but he confirmed it once we made eye contact. I tapped Phe-Phe on her arm, interrupting her discussion. I nodded my head over to the man and asked, "What do I do?"

Phe-Phe laughed out loud, grabbed my hand, and led me over to the bar.

"Iyana, this is Michael Eubanks. Michael, this is Iyana. Michael is one of the lawyers working on my case. He and his twin practice together. I told them briefly about you this morning, and he wanted to come by and meet you himself."

Completely embarrassed, I lowered my head and gave him a weak hello.

"I understand, young lady that you are in a foreign place and may not use to men offering you drinks in a club, but just remember I am completely harmless." He flashed me a big smile and handed Phe Phe and I a Red Stripe beer. Even though he too had an accent, his had more of a British tone.

She took the drink from him and planted a kiss on his cheek. I looked around the room and watched all the women winding their bodies to the groove of the music. I used to watch my mother dance like this from time to time when we were alone at home, but she made me promise to never tell my father.

From that statement, I always thought it had to be something wrong if we had to keep it a secret, but I would be lying if I told you that the movements didn't fascinate me. And to now, watching all the ladies in here gyrating their hips was almost beautiful.

I don't know how long I was in my own world before Phe Phe nudged me.

"You, okay?"

I nodded, yes, never taking my eyes off of the dance floor.

"They look nice, huh? Well, that's what I wanted to talk to you about. Where we are is not only a club, but also considered to be a dance hall, and the baddest, tightest dancer in the place is considered to be a dancehall queen. The beauty of a dancehall queen is indescribable. We tell a story with our body all the while possessing sex appeal."

A dancehall queen. Just the other day Aunt Madge was watching a VHS tape of a movie called "Dancehall Queen." The part I walked in on was when Marcia, the main character, was at home in the mirror trying to dance, but looked like a complete fool. That's going to be me if I did go along with this plan.

"Don't frown upon us," Phe Phe continued. "Secretly, a lot of women wish that they were one of us. There are contests all the time that are held for money that give you a chance to prove you are the dancehall queen. In D.C., I won $10,000, so just think of what you would get here."

One of us? She won? Was she a dancehall queen? Was she thinking about teaching me to become one too?

Before I could share with her my thoughts, the host got on the mic and said, "We have a celebrity in the house today! Please welcome mi frien, mi Sista, Phe!"

Phe handed me her drink telling me, "Watch and learn how to use your pum pum the right way," and sauntered to the stage. She bounced to the music with every step, hyping the crowd up. By the time she reached the stage, the crowd was going wild. The music was pumping so hard that I even started to sway to the beat.

Phe Phe jumped on the stage and immediately stood on her head with her backside facing the audience.

She started to do something that was a cross between of American twerking and booty popping. The crowd went bananas. I kept a smile on my face, watching her roll into the splits, doing the same motion with her ass for a few seconds before rolling her hips back up into a standing position.

I had a talented new friend that kept me in awe. I continued to watch her show and think at the same time. *10,000 bucks?*

I think I can do it, I thought. *Well, as long as Phe-Phe was going to be patient with me.*

The Eubanks Brothers

Mason

I pulled my BMW into the adjoining parking lot of Club Quad. I wasn't usually the one to go club-hopping, but Phe Phe stressed the importance that I met her new friend and our new potential client. My girlfriend, Neka, was so excited, and her eyes were full of it. Popcaan, one her favorite reggae artists, was going to perform tonight. I usually chose to stay at home while she went out to enjoy her night in the town, so she was happy to have me in her arms tonight.

It has been at least nine months since the last time we had a night in the town. Ever since we bumped into the man, she was cheating on me with during a Reggae Sun Splash event, I opted out on having the pleasure of meeting another one of her beaus.

I know it sounds awkward, hearing one say that they know their partner was cheating, but I know all about her infidelities. She swore up and down that she was faithful to me, but the streets were talking. Neka looked good in my arms and knew the lingo to hold her own when I frequented certain political events, but that was it. I stopped sleeping with her after that, but like the saying goes, it is cheaper to keep her.

I paid the parking attendant and followed his instructions on where to park. The humidity outside blew across my face as I held Neka's hand and escorted her into the front of the club.

Even though there was a line wrapped around the building, I wasn't worried about getting in. My brother and I were well-known in New Kingston for the work we do, saving deportees and fighting for injustices. Even while I guided her to the door, Neka couldn't keep her eyes off of the men that were in line, constantly flashing each one a bright smile.

I kept a firm grip on her hand and gently pulled her the remaining way to the entrance. Neka turned to smile at the man at the door and motioned with her lips that she was going to come back in a few minutes. I shook my head at her.

Noticing that she was beginning to upset me, she quickly apologized, poking her bottom lip out. A few years ago, I would have cared about her getting upset and pouting, but now, I didn't care. Sometimes, her approach reminded me of a desperate man trying to fuck the next best thing.

"You are a bloody asshole," I mumbled under my breath, upset that she was acting a fool, and we hadn't even reached our party yet.

Once inside, I'd let her go free, so she could do whatever the hell it was that she pleased. Before I could give the bouncer my name, he greeted me with a big smile, "Hello, Mr. Eubanks! Your brother is already inside."

As soon as the wristbands were on our wrists, I let Neka go, handing her a wad of money. "Have fun, love," I told her, eager to get her out of my sight.

Instantly, her frown turned into a smile as she looked around. I nodded my head to the music. She spotted one of her girlfriends, and she was gone into the crowd.

I was about to head to the bar when the music stopped, and the DJ introduced Phe Phe to the floor. I stopped and watched her dance on that stage as if her body was nothing. I loved seeing Caribbean women dance, especially Jamaican women. When my brother decided to move our firm to Jamaica from the UK, this was one of the highlights of the move.

We were born in Jamaica, but our mother moved us to England when we were about four years old. Our mother worked so hard to get us through law school, but she did it.

It wasn't until she died that we both realized that England was not a home without her. We could provide humanitarian services and make money to the country we were products of, so we decided to move back to Jamaica. I brought Neka over with me, and I used to think she was going to be my wife, but this move allowed me to see her true colors.

There were a series of cheers and clapping that rang out throughout the club once Phe Phe was finished. I continued my trek to the bar. I knew that after that performance, my friend was going to need a drink. The DJ started the music again as people began to make their way back to the dance floor.

Before I reached the bar, I spotted my brother chatting with a beautiful, curly-haired woman. *Is this the friend that Phe Phe wanted us to meet?* I had to get my thoughts and my cool together before I went over there, stumbling over my words.

This was the woman whose fiancé had set her up to be deported and stole her entire inheritance? Who would want her to be alone in the world? Of course, we were going to help her. She didn't need any money right now! I will pay her retainer to my brother myself. I just need to be able to see her again.

I got it together and finished my trek to the bar. My brother spotted me and gave me the biggest hug.

"She's beautiful," he whispered to me, not wanting anyone else to hear. "She is also intelligent. Maybe her being here will allow you to let go of Neka and think about a real woman."

Smiling, I patted my brother on the back and laughed. Even though he was almost 100 pounds heavier than me, we still looked just alike and could read each other's thoughts.

I patted him on the back and broke our embrace. I didn't know why, but my heart was beginning to skip a beat. *Yes, she is beautiful,* but there was something else about her that made me want her, lust for her, need to protect her.

"Miss Iyana, this is my brother, Mason. Iyana's father was a partner of a firm in Florida before he died. I was just telling her how great minds think alike."

Grabbing Iyana's left hand, I brought it to my lips and brushed a soft kiss across it before I gave her a big smile.

"Nice to meet you, Iyana. Phe Phe has already explained to us your plight, and we are going to do everything in our power to get you back to the States."

Iyana smiled back at me, blushing at the same time. She stood around 5' 4, but that didn't stop all her confidence from shining out through her. It was indescribable.

"So, I see that you have met your new client," Phe Phe said, hugging Iyana from the side. She was right on cue, pulling her to the dance floor. Michael and I watched the pair saunter over to the dance floor, both of them swaying their hips to the beat. I was confident that Phe Phe was going to be able to teach her everything she needed to know to start winning competitions. Phe Phe has always gone after what she wanted, and by any means necessary, she always ended up winning.

I stood on the sidelines and watched the pair dance in the middle of the crowd. Even with Iyana wearing that sundress, hanging all the way down to her feet, all the men on the floor wanted a moment to dance with her. The two of them immediately became the life of the party, dancing and laughing at each other as if they were old friends.

My brother handed me a drink and nodded his head. "So, it's confirmed we have a new client, correct?" I nodded back and smiled. I was really excited to work with her... for more reasons than she would ever know.

Research

Phe Phe

"Hello, my name is Phoebe Jamison, and I wanted to know if Bradley Hinkle was available?"

I was sitting in my living room with a pen and pencil in my hand, waiting for the receptionist to come back and take the message for me. Michael and I came up with a plan to find out some of the behind-scene information on what really happened to Iyana.

All it took to kick it off was to have Michael's assistant call and request a copy of Iyana's deportation file. There was a little bit of information that was conveniently left out and not told to Iyana. Information such as, there was a person that actually contacted the ICE and reported that Iyana was recently convicted of a crime. Also, after she was arrested, Bradley informed the police that he believed she was a part of a drug trafficking ring. He didn't feel comfortable testifying against her, but he wanted the officers to know what type of person they were dealing with.

I have decided to call Bradley every day, posing as a representative of Iyana's legal team requesting that he provide funding for our services and information.

The young lady on the receiving end of the phone jotted down my information, informing me that she was going to have Mr. Hinkle call me back. Apparently, he was still in court.

"Okay, that is fine. Can you make sure to let him know that we are re-opening his client's/fiancé's case from Jamaica to overturn her deportation, and it is very important that we speak to him? Bye now."

I went into my sitting room and sat down at the table. I had so many papers sprawled across the table, full of information on Bradley. I found out a lot about who the real Bradley is and how many different women he had been with, many of which had ended up in similar situations as Iyana. This man thinks he is invincible, but I am one with nothing to lose, so I have no problem seeing this through to the end.

Moments like these, it wasn't a bad thing that I lived alone. If I had a nosy husband snooping around, my goal would not be obtainable.

As much as I didn't want to, my heart had started shedding its walls and letting Iyana in. There was something about her from day one, and I just felt the need to protect her. So far, she is actually doing pretty well with our dance lessons, slowly preparing her for battle. We practiced three to four days a week, going over new and old dance hall moves.

It's only been a month, but I think she's about ready to go out onto the stage alone. We have been going from club to club almost every night, allowing her to get to know some of the other dance hall queens and watch some of the tricks that they do.

I want Iyana to feel at home and begin to feel comfortable all the way around. I know my friend is feeling all alone as if Bradley abandoned her. However, after he starts receiving these phone calls, explaining what we were doing with Iyana's case, I know for a fact that I am going to be hearing from him soon.

He was not ready for the wrath that I was piecing together to unleash upon him. Iyana deserved the best, and from what I could see about Bradley, he was far from it.

Hmmmm, I thought to myself, flipping through the pages. *This arresting officer has put away two of Bradley's girls. I wonder if he had any information to tell me.*

I wrote his name and number under the U.S. police information I had written onto a pad and continued to go through my documentation, building my case against Bradley.

Preparation

Iyana

When I agreed to have Phe Phe dress me for my first time out on the dance floor, I thought she was going to take me to her house and pick out something for me to wear. Instead, she insisted that we go shopping in Downtown Kingston to find something. I wasn't too happy about running up my tab with her, but she didn't care.

"We got the dance down," she said. "Now, you have to look the part."

It felt like hours as we went in and out of different shopping malls, trying on so many articles of clothing. I have always been a modest person, so having me try on dresses with studs on the breasts, or dresses with holes everywhere, but my vagina and butt, was only making me want to run for cover, instead of embracing Jamaica's version of American hip-hop culture. I know I was driving Phe Phe crazy, but I had to at least feel comfortable in the clothing that was going to cover my body and not worry about it falling off of me. I was about to give up when Phe Phe yelled out, "I got it! Spicy Couture!"

I followed her up the stairs and into a boutique that actually had more of a selection than the ones we went into before. Phe Phe went crazy, picking out items for me with a melancholy look on her face.

"Where you ladies going tonight on a Tuesday?" an older man, which was there with two women, asked me.

"Ummmm, I am not too sure. I think to a dance hall party." Before I could finish answering, Phe Phe interrupted us.

"This is Jamaica, sir. There is always something going on. There is never a dull moment in Jamaica." She laughed out loud, while handing me a pair of red tights. "Try this on with this jacket."

I held the pieces up together, waiting for her to give me a tank top.

Catching the confusion on my face, Phe Phe laughed again, shaking her head. "I am not exactly sure what you are waiting for. You are going to just put on a red or black brazier underneath."

"Ugh-uh, Phe! I am going to be naked!"

I had to admit the thin, tan blazer jacket with the red tights actually looked cute together, but I have never just worn a bra out in public! I don't even go swimming in a two piece. I know that I am desperate right now, but to change who I am.... I wasn't too sure. I have already lost everything, but now I have to lose my sense of respect too.

Before I had a chance to plead my case, my cellphone rang. Laughing out loud, I dug it out of my purse and dropped it on the ground when I checked the caller ID.

Bradley? That was Bradley's number on my phone. Why was he calling now? Where have he been all this time?

"What's wrong, girl! You crazy? You haven't made any money yet to be breaking up the little stuff that you got."

Phe Phe came over to find out what was wrong. Bending down, she picked up my phone, but I wouldn't let her answer.

"I- I- It's Bradley, and I don't know what to say to him?"

Phe Phe stared at me as if I as crazy.

"What do you mean, 'you don't know what to say to him?' You ask that fucker why he thieved away your shit! Hold on, I will ask him for you!"

She checked the caller ID to call him back. I have never seen Phe Phe so mad. Her face was turning red as she tried to get him back on the phone.

"No Phe, let me handle this. I will call him back, but when I am ready to talk."

Even though the words were coming out of my mouth, my feelings were the exact opposite. I had been dreaming of this day, but I needed to speak to Bradley in private. I did not know what direction this conversation was going to go into, but I didn't want to do it in front of anyone, especially Phe Phe.

"Well said, little Sista!"

Phe Phe grabbed my hand, dragging me to the dressing room.

"I know just what you need to take your mind off of things.... Trying on these pretty-pretty clothes I am picking out."

Laughing out loud, I let go of my frustrations and followed my friend. Eventually, I was going to have that much needed conversation with Bradley, but not by his command. From now on, everything was going to be on my terms.

Disbelief

Bradley

Iyana sent me a voicemail. What the fuck is going on? It has been almost seven months since I have seen her, and I am not going to lie, I did kind of miss her. You spend so many years with a person, you get used to them, and everything that they do for you, but watching my plan unfold every time made my dick hard. Everything fell into its place, and I was happy at the ending results.

They always talk about how strong and proud black women are— and they are, but once you get them like putty in the palm of your hands, you can get them to do the impossible. Don't get me wrong. I started to love Iyana. I was always attracted to her, even when she was a young girl I wanted her, but I was never *in love* with her.

She was the weakest one out of all of the women I have had over the last fifteen years, but she was the wealthiest. Her father gave that girl a silver spoon in her mouth, and she was such an airhead that she didn't even know it. Spoiled bitches like her drove me crazy, so every time something stupid came out of her mouth in regard to finances, it didn't make me feel bad for the next account I would have her sign authority of to me. My uncle really wanted me to stop trafficking drugs, and I know I needed to, but the high I am on during the process felt just as good as making these girls believe in me.

Back when I set up Natasha, my first island girlfriend, it wasn't for a high. It was going to be me or her, and I just couldn't allow that to happen. Natasha, just like the others, went back to her country and stayed there peacefully. Of course, I got occasional calls in the past, but after I changed my number, which was all she wrote.

This time was different because I was actually working in a firm that was named after Iyana's father, so she had access to get in contact with me. But the plan has been working so well, I wasn't prepared for the constant calls I've been getting from Ms. Phoebe. I could not lie. Hearing Phoebe's voice on my voicemail turned me on so badly that pre-cum would leak out. I was in love with the accents. As badly as I wanted to hear her talk to me, I needed to speak to Iyana first to see exactly what was going on.

The disconnect from her heritage is what I didn't understand. She was actually born there and didn't know anything about it. That was the part about Iyana that I could not stand. She did not have an accent at all. Not even one that came out when she was around other Jamaicans. She barely understood their dialect as it is. That was another reason why I was okay with her getting up out of here.

Shaking my head, images of her being arrested inside of our home flashed in front of my eyes. She was terrified, which started to scare me. I didn't think they would send her all the way back to Jamaica because her charge was brought down to a misdemeanor. I was sure they were just going to make her serve time within their facility for a couple of months, like they did one of my old girls, Hannah. That would have given me enough time to take enough money for me to be cool. I could've told her that I couldn't be with her anymore because she had a record, and that wouldn't look good for my image.

That was the only reason I made the anonymous call to ICE a couple of days after she went to court. I just knew how this was going to play out, but once they said she was going to be deported back to Jamaica, I knew I had to cut off all ties. If I had supported her, it was possible that they could have come after me and my underground drug operation.

So, now to know that Iyana managed to obtain legal representation that has offices in America, Europe, and Jamaica, my mind can't get it together. Hell, I was shocked that she was able to get a cell phone— and that quickly. I needed to know exactly what it was they knew. I listened to all of Iyana's messages, and even up until now, she still sounds sad, confused, and in love.

I dialed her number again and again; it went to voicemail. Hmmm.

I picked up my phone once more, this time calling my uncle. His phone only rang half a time before he picked up.

"Did you talk to her yet?" he asked, not saying hello.

His voice was full of apprehension, which scared the shit out of me.

"Nope, not yet."

I knew exactly why he was paranoid, the same reason that I was. If I went down, he was going down. He was just as much involved in my organization as I was, so it was very important for us to talk to her quickly.

"You know you are going to have to get her back on your side, Bradley," his voice was stern and strong.

"Yes, sir," I replied. "Let me give you a call back. I hear the garage opening."

Quickly, I hung up the phone and turned down the volume of the ringer.

"Baby are you home?" a soft Latin voice called out from downstairs.

"Yes, I am *mamacita*, waiting for you to put your pretty mouth around Daddy's dick."

I heard her giggle, but I knew she knew what time it was. I needed something to release this tension and quick. I unbuckled my pants and headed down the stairs. I always think better with a clear head.

Pretty Brown Eyes

Mason

"I am about to head out of here, Mason. Is there anything else you want to go over before I leave?"

My brother was standing in the doorway of my office, rubbing his forehead. We have been working non-stop, trying to formulate a plan to get Iyana home. The late nights and early mornings were starting to get to both of us, but we are both stubborn creatures by nature and would not stop until we get what we want.

"What time are you going to be heading out of here?" he asked, glancing at his watch.

I shook my head, looking down at my desk. I have so much going on that it may be well after midnight that I leave here. With Phe Phe's help, there has been so many loopholes within the body of this case that it was ridiculous. We were able to obtain a court date a couple of weeks away to have Iyana's case brought before the Immigration Department.

I watched my brother prep to leave. I knew the real reason why he was trying to get out of here. He had a date and didn't want to be late.

"Have fun, big brother. I will make sure to lock up behind me, and let you know."

"See you in the morning. Have a good night." I heard Michael call, heading out the door.

Iyana was so damn strong. Ever since I met her, the air of protection just circles around her, engulfing me. She was so quiet and reserved, but if you pissed her off, she could turn into a firecracker. Stranded on an island where it is apparent, she is not from, she doesn't let it discourage here. She worked so hard, filling in the pieces that would have been all that I needed.

There was a soft knocking sound outside the office door. I turned on the main light in the reception area and opened the door. I was startled, but happy when I opened the door and set eyes upon Iyana.

"Hey there!" I said, welcoming her in. "It is always a lovely day any chance I get to see you." I just saw her this morning and was not expecting a second opportunity to lay eyes upon her. It was so hard to keep her off my mind, and now here she is, standing right in front of me. She is so damn beautiful, but right now, there is something different about her. Something in her eyes made me feel eerie.

"Hey, you," Iyana said, gradually running her hands down her thighs.

"Is there something wrong, pretty girl? You seem preoccupied."

She stood on her tip toes and kissed my cheek. Her intimate gesture startled me, making me take a couple of steps back into my office. That was all I needed as an invitation. My mind wanted to lift her up, carry her to my desk, and make love to her beautiful body, but I was trying so damn hard to do the opposite. At times, it felt like Iyana cared about me too, but at other times, you can see that here heart was somewhere else.

Even though Michael, Phe Phe, and I have uncovered a lot, we have been selective on what we chose to tell her. We knew that eventually she was going to talk to Bradley, especially since we had been contacting him non-stop, trying to find out what was going on. We were trying to bring him out of hiding, and by the look on her face, our plan may have worked.

I sat down at my desk and just admired her. Just like that old song, "Beauty" is her name, which is how I felt about her. She was so delicate like a flower, and I loved watching her bloom. Being around Phe Phe, she was becoming stronger and stronger every day.

Iyana, not saying anything, stood right in front of my chair and ran her hands up and down my chest.

My heart was beating uncontrollably. I felt as if I was having an outer body experience. I wanted to push her away from me, remind her that she was my client, but the words were caught inside my throat. It has been awhile since I have been touched intimately by a woman, and my body was going out of control. My eyes rolled to the back of my head as Iyana straddled me and leaned in to kiss me. The kiss that we shared was so sweet, so slow. She teased the outside of my lips with her tongue, causing my toes to curl. She made love to my mouth with her tongue biting, licking, and tasting me.

"Iyana, please stop it!"

Even though I wanted to see just how far we could go, I did not want this to happen because she was upset about her ex. If, and when, we finally made love, it would be something sweet, beautiful, and memorable.

"Baby, please," I whispered in between kisses. Even though my mouth requested for her to top, my body was still responding.

Iyana broke our embrace, throwing her head into my chest. If she didn't stop it, I wasn't too sure if I was going to be able too.

I ran my fingers through her curls and kissed her eyebrows, hairline, and cheeks.

"Bradley called, but I didn't say anything to him," she said into my chest between sobs. "Just seeing his number flash across my caller ID scared me."

I listened to her pour her heart out about Bradley, how she once wanted to have his name, how she wanted to experience the big church wedding. She was hurt, but the realization that he only called because Phe Phe had been blowing up his phone made Iyana feel even more angry. She wanted to hate him badly, but her heart would not let her.

Instead of taking advantage of Iyana, (like I wanted too) I held her close and tried my best to soothe her. I wanted her so badly, but I didn't want to be another one of the men on her list that made her heart hurt. I wanted to be the man that made her smile every day.

Movin'

Iyana

"I still can't believe that I'm about to do this," I said to Phe Phe. My body was shaking as I stood at the bar with Phe Phe, waiting for it to be my turn. She had arranged for one of her friends from the states, GQ, to come and perform while I danced. She figured that it would be easier for me to perform if I danced to a song that I already knew, and "Movin'" was a fast, upbeat Dancehall song.

I flashed the bartender my left hand to remind her that I needed another drink. This was going to be my third drink of the night, and I still did not have a buzz at all.

According to Phe Phe, the club was on point and the drinks were cut, so I needed to make sure that my performance stood out. The music began:

When the sun go down, the moon come out, the dance hall queen in me want to get out, out, out out, out, in my pum pum shorts....

That was my queue! I skipped to the stage, winding my body as I took to the center. It took a moment for the crowd to catch on to what I was doing, but by the time GQ sang out, "All my dance hall queens hit the floor!" I was on the stage.

I closed my eyes and did everything I had practiced at home with Phe Phe. I loved the song because the beat was hot and made you want to move. With my eyes closed, I could see my mother dancing in the kitchen, and I pretended to be her.

I don't know if the crowd was cheering for me or for GQ because she was dancing just as hard as I was. Her band, Euro Trash Collective, may have been a bunch of white boys, but they were getting it! That is what I loved about Caribbean music. It didn't mattered what background, social class, or ethnicity you came from.

When you heard the music, you wanted to get up and dance, just like GQ's lyrics, just like me on this stage.

I stuck my thumbs into the top of my shorts and ticked my lower body to the music all the way to the ground. I turned around, so that my ass was facing the audience. Still ticking on the ground, I jumped up and landed into a split still on the beat. I don't know where this person came from, but I loved how free I allowed myself to be.

The crowd started chanting: Pum Pum, Pum Pum, Pum Pum! The adrenaline just made me dance harder. I did every dancehall dance that Phe Phe taught me from "the Shook It Up," "the Tun Up," and "the Calm Step." When I heard the song begin to end, I danced my ass off the stage and into the crowd, just like we practiced. Everyone was trying to dance with me! It didn't matter who it was—man or woman. I continued my routine until I was at the bar, and I struck my poise.

I was panting like an old dog, but the crowd gave me a standing ovation! I couldn't stop laughing! Phe Phe told me to do the damn thing, and I did the damn thing! I was very proud of myself.

Phe Phe ran up to me and hugged me so damn tight. "You did that, Sista!" she yelled out at me.

"Well, I wouldn't have been able to do anything if I didn't have a great teacher!" We hugged, and that's when I noticed there was a line starting to form.

They lining up? Is for me?

I was not ready for this kind of attention, but I am not going to lie to you, it felt damn good! The DJ was back on the mic, thanking all the contestants for being a part of the event.

"So, you know it's about that time to announce the winner, but I think all of you already know who the winner is." He paused for a moment and screamed out... "And the winner is Iyana, aka Pum Pum!!!!"

I heard him, but I couldn't believe that I heard him correctly. Not only did he come down to where I was, he handed me my new trophy and 100,000 Jamaican dollars! I didn't know what to do or to say. *I did it!* The tears flowed from my eyes as Mason wrapped his arms around me. Phe

Phe came running to the bar, bawling her damn self.

"I am so proud of you!" Phe Phe said, hugging Mason and me.

I don't know how long we embrace before Phe Phe said, "Hey... Let's go. We still dealing with fools. We don't need you to get robbed, Ms. Pum Pum."

We all laughed and headed out. Tonight, was going down in history as one of the best nights of my life.

Tomorrow is Never Promised
Phe Phe

Sitting down at the kitchen table, munching on banana, I was going through the Kingston Gazette. Even though it has been over a week since Iyana won the dancehall contest, she was still popping up in the newspaper. I felt like a proud parent every time I saw her pretty face in the paper or on the news broadcast on television.

She deserved every moment of it. She was starting to live for today, and I loved watching her morph into this beautiful being right before my eyes.

Ding! The message alert on my phone went off, startling me.

Flight leaves two weeks from today. PW official. I will email you the itinerary. M.

I sent him a quick *kk* and a happy face.

I was ready for this trip. Mason and I decided that we were going to have to take matters into our own hands to protect Iyana— I mean, Pum Pum. LOL, I still can't believe that was the name they gave her.

Chuckling, my phone went off again. This time it was Iyana calling.

"Wuh gwan!" I greeted her with a big smile on my face, but the piercing scream that came from her throat scared me.

"Aunt Madge is gone Phe! Who do I have now? My aunt is gone!" she cried out between wails. I tried to calm her down, but I couldn't. She didn't hear anything I had to say.

I hung up the phone and dressed in lightning speed to get to my friend's side. I knew that tomorrow was not promised to anyone, but damn. Didn't this girl deserve a break?

Just the thought of it makes my plans even more valid. I was going to handle Bradley later. Right now, it was my time to be there for Iyana.

Chaquita

Phe Phe

Sitting on the plane, I watched the clip from the movie "Belly," where Chaquita comes to America to murder Ox. He betrayed his drug family back in Jamaica, so he had to meet the piper. The same exact approach that Chaquita had when she used the element of surprise to slit Ox's throat from ear to ear is the same game tactic that I am about to use on this fool.

I wanted him to pay and die a slow, painful death. I needed him to know that the moment he took his last breath he was going through this because of Iyana.

I studied the packet that Detective Brown sent to Mason. It had everything about Bradley in one file. There were pictures from different angles of him, his home address, the makes and models of all vehicles registered to him and Iyana, and his office location. When I saw that Iyana's name was still on the house and most of the vehicles, it pissed me off even more. This fool didn't even have the decency to take things out of her name. While she was residing in Tivoli Gardens, one of the poorest garrisons in Kingston, he was living the high life with his new bitch of the week?

"Ladies and gentlemen, please fasten your seat belts. Make sure that all trays are in an upright position, and prepare for landing," the stewardess announced over the intercom. This is the first time I have been back in America since I was deported.

My situation was totally different from Iyana's. I wasn't sad when I was sentenced to a one-way trip back to Jamaica. Actually, I pressed my legal team to get that done instead of me spending any time in a D.C. prison. As you can see, I am a firm believer in an eye for an eye.

I considered myself to be a good person and thought I had lived my life the right way. So, to find out that the person I loved the most, the one I would do anything for, the one that I thought loved me the most, had given me HIV, which gradually progressed into full-blown AIDS, I saw red. I thought, hell, if I am dying anyway, I might as well take him out with me.

I plotted for a month on when it was going to be the perfect time to even bring it up to him. I assumed he was going to do the typical man thing and deny it. Claim that the doctors were wrong, hell, even blame me for giving it to him. But no, he did the exact opposite.

When I confronted Jason about infecting me, he didn't deny it. His only response was short and simple, "I just found out as well. I didn't know. Well, at least I have enough money to take care of us together. You have to always look at the bright side."

Next, he kissed me on the cheek, slapped me on the ass, and told me to go fix him some breakfast. His nonchalant attitude angered the hell out of me. I went downstairs, made him breakfast, and brought it back upstairs like a good wife on a tray. I tried to sit it down across his lap, but he didn't want that. Instead, he motioned for me to put it on the dresser and come to him.

Coming back to bed, Jason ran his fingers through my hair. The gesture used to make my insides weak, but not today. This man was blowing my mind. Right after we have a conversation about having HIV, he wants to have sex. Who does that one?

He pulled me to down to straddle his lap as he leaned into part my lips with his tongue. He whispered sweet nothings in between kisses, which disgusted me. Chills ran through my body, but the kind of delight. It was a feeling I had never felt before. It was a sensation full of rage!

I couldn't believe this man was trying to make love to me. I used to want him so badly, but now, his touch made my skin crawl. My sun rose and set to that man, and he knew it.

Raising the thin material of my gown, Jason Anthony gathered my full breasts within his palms and played with my nipples. I threw my head back, full of adrenaline and hate. My heart was beating rapidly, my breath running wild, and the feeling that I was feeling inside was something that I never experienced before, and it scared the shit out of me.

Once the warmth of his tongue reached my quarter shaped nipples, I froze. The touching and teasing that he was doing with his tongue and hands was supposed to be driving me crazy, but it was doing the exact opposite.

Before I allowed him to enter either one of my holes, I needed to do something quickly because I knew what was coming next. I leaned over and grabbed the steak knife off tray and began stabbing him in the chest with it. The look on his face was priceless after he realized that he was being assaulted.

I stabbed him over and over again until the last bit of life inside of his body drifted away. I continued to straddle his lap, attempting to calm myself down. His blood was everywhere from the bed to the walls, on our floor, and most definitely, all over me. My first thought was to get up and clean myself up, but I didn't. Still straddled across his lap, I leaned over, picked up the phone, and dialed my bank.

I transferred all our money out of our accounts and into my personal one. Once that was complete, I called the police.

The mistake and blessing that I made killing Jason, is that I did it full of rage. It made it appear that I snapped, and it turned into a crime of passion which in turn got me deported and not cooped up in someone's jail cell going crazy.

When we landed, I got off the plane and headed straight to the Customs Department. The fake visa and passport that I had come straight from the Jamaican embassy and was not a cheap replica, like most of the immigrants possessed when they tried to migrate illegally.

"Thank you, Ms. Henry," the customs officer told me, flashing me a huge smile. "I hope you enjoy your stay in Florida."

Nodding, I smiled and made my way to baggage claim.

July 4, 2014

Happy Anniversary
Bradley

Finally, Iyana called me back! It wasn't the conversation I wanted to hear because she was upset. Apparently, her great-aunt had passed away, but as crazy as it may sound, it felt good to hear her voice. According to Iyana, even though her aunt lived very modestly, Iyana's late mother had arranged to pay for her funeral arrangements years ago, just in case anything ever happened.

Iyana was so upset; I almost didn't have the opportunity to ask her about her legal team.

"Since I couldn't get in contact with you, I had to register for some local programs where the lawyers fight pro-bono to try to save you. Have you spoken to them?"

At first, I was going to lie to her and tell her yes, but for what? I felt a little better because if they were working pro-bono, I doubted they were going to do an extensive check to find out what was going on.

"Bradley, what happened to us?" she questioned after taking a deep breath. I sat in silence on the phone because I really didn't have a valid answer for her. I had practiced my story for weeks now in the event that or when I had the chance to speak to her, but now that I had her on the phone in the present, I was tongue tied.

Iyana must have felt hesitant, and she quickly excused herself off the phone. She hung up so quickly, not even saying bye. I was debating whether or not to call her back when Daisy popped her head into the room.

"You about ready, baby?" she asked me. Daisy was my chick for the moment, and she knew it. Even though she was Brazilian, thick, and beautiful, I think she enjoyed other people's pussy just as much as me.

I had fun in bed with Daisy, but outside of that, we had nothing else in common.

"Yes, baby. I am about ready to go. Let me finish this call really quickly. Meet you in the garage."

I unlocked the doors to Iyana's Porsche and watched her get inside. I used to unlock the passenger door for Iyana, but now since she was gone, the gentleman in me left as well.

Unlike Iyana who was very low-key, Daisy was the total opposite. If she could, she would be inside the walls of someone's club every night. I promised her a night out in the town for the holiday. I needed to do something different to get the thought of last year's fiasco out of my head, so I took her to Gerald's Bar and Lounge. They had good food, drinks, hookah, and they were even going to do their own fireworks show, so there was something there for both of us.

Daisy was sitting back in the seat with her right arm hanging out of the window. We drove in silence. I already knew what was on her mind. She loved this car so much and didn't care that it used to belong to my ex—she wanted it.

One person's trash is the next person's treasure, the old saying goes. I know I sound crazy, considering everything I put Iyana through, but I still didn't feel comfortable letting Daisy drive this car, let alone *giving* it to her. Now that I had spoken to Iyana, I felt especially crazy having another woman inside of her car. But I guess another old saying applies here, *out of sight, out of mind.*

After hearing Iyana's voice that day, I really didn't know why, but I was actually feeling guilty. Another thing that was bothering me was that Iyana never asked for anything: clothes, personal items, money. How was she surviving? I knew that she was being short and sweet because it was an international call, but she didn't share anything with me besides the death of her aunt.

Pulling up in front of the bar, I waited for the valet to come and let us out. Trying to get Iyana out of my mind was hard because I did miss her. Hearing her voice brought back all kinds of pent-up emotions for her.

A smile crept up the corners of my mouth as I watched a beautiful, brown-skinned woman exit the car in front of me. Her long, jet-black hair was shiny and straight. The red dress she wore was hugging and covering her in all the right places. She glanced inside the car and smiled at both of us. I assume to take that smile as an open invitation. She was the first thing I was going to check for once inside the bar.

Five hours later, we were playing truth or dare while drinking patron. I didn't take her for being a woman that liked women, but she was here with us. Daisy had convinced her to come back home with us, and not for me.

Rocci was the name of our new friend, and I was excited. She was Dominican and just my type! I knew how Daisy could be, so I let her play with her first: touching her hair, running her hands over her hips. I watched the pair dance on the floor together. Their movements were so damn sexy to me. Once, I caught Daisy running her fingertips over Rocci's breast, and the latter responded by winding her hips closer into Daisy while we were still at the club. I couldn't wait to get them both home and enjoy this live entertainment. Listening and watching the cuddling and carrying on was becoming too much.

I didn't know exactly what Rocci was doing to Daisy in the backseat, but I could tell by the giggling and moaning that they needed some privacy, but I didn't care. What about me! As soon as I pulled into the driveway, I hopped out and opened the front door, so I could quickly usher them in.

Daisy was so wasted that she kept messing up and losing the game. Every time someone messed up, they had to remove a particle from clothing. Daisy only had on her panties. Rocci was still fully dressed though. She was playing too well, and I needed her to start losing soon.

Daisy went to the bathroom and came back with a candy dish filled with coke.

"She just needs to relax. Here, come take a hit with me."

I watched her roll up a twenty-dollar bill and went to town on her drugs. Once she was finished, I motioned for Rocci to come get some.

Shaking her head, she politely declined. Instead, she lifted her dress and pulled it up and over her head.

I watched her stand there, wearing only panties. She held such a peaceful demeanor that turned me on. Not only was she beautiful, but she wasn't a drughead, like Daisy. That was another thing I admired about Iyana; I never even saw her lift a cigarette to her lips.

UGH!!! WHY DID MY MIND KEEP GOING BACK TO HER! I NEEDED TO GET IT TOGETHER AND HAVE FUN WITH THESE TWO BEAUTIFUL MAIDENS IN FRONT OF ME.

"Papi, I'm ready even if she isn't."

Daisy straddled me, leaning in kissing my top lip, and then my bottom.

Excited, my response was to pour some coke onto her chest and snorted it straight up across her titties. The drugs burned my chest and made me more excited. Between kisses, I continued to watch Rocci, hoping that she would come and join us.

"Let me just watch you two first," she said. "When you are finished, I promise you I am going to join in." I flipped Daisy over, positioning her bent over the bed, so that I could have full access to watch Rocci watch me.

Cupping my pecs, I made her back arch as I shoved my dick inside of her. I don't know if it was the drugs, her instant wetness, or the fact that Rocci was watching us while rubbing on her mound that excited me, but I was ready to get to round two quickly.

My body was trembling as I continued to pound out her insides, staring deeply into Rocci's intense eyes.

Moments later, I felt myself climax as I screamed out in delight. The session was so good that Daisy immediately fell asleep in the same position, bent over the edge of the bed.

I fell to the ground, my heart pounding in my chest.

"What are you thinking?" I asked her, smiling mischievously. I was ready to get this show back on the road and see what the island of Dominica felt like.

Flashing a bright smile at me, Rocci asked, "Do you mind if I go get some ice? I love to use props to set the mood. Is that okay with you?"

"Of course," I replied, lying flat on my back, folding my hands across my chest.

Not saying another word, Rocci hurried out of the room and down the stairs. After a few minutes, I felt her presence coming closer, making the hairs on the back of my neck stand up in excitement. I kept my eyes closed, waiting to feel the coolness of the ice impact my body.

A loud moan escaped my throat as she leaned closer and rubbed my chest. I don't know why, but I wanted this one so fucking badly that it was pathetic.

"Are you ready?" she asked me, barely above a whisper.

I nodded, yes, in excitement squeezing my eyes closed even tighter.

Instead of the pleasure that I was building up to receive, I wasn't prepared for the sharp pain that struck my neck. I opened my eyes to see Rocci strike me again with a hammer.

"Happy Anniversary, bitch!" she yelled at me, smashing the hammer again against my rib cage.

The pain was so excruciating that I couldn't even scream out in agony. As hard as I tried, no sound would come out.

"You can't scream because I smashed your vocal chords first. All day I've been thinking and thinking: what is it that I can do to make you feel the same kind of pain and agony that you put her through? This is for Iyana. I hate men like you. You want to take and control the life of women. Well, let me control and take yours."

She continued to beat me with the hammer over and over again until finally, I watched her swing the hammer towards my head. The last thing I remembered was trying to close my eyes, but it was too late. That last impact took my life.

Somebody Pray for Me
Iyana

Father God in Heaven,

I come to you with the most sincerity in my heart. May you please watch over me and remove all this pain and hurt from my heart. Please, Father God, heal me and bless me. I need you more now than I ever have, Lord. God, I see the work that you have done within me, and my life and I know that you don't make any mistakes, but after you took my Aunt Madge from me as well, I am starting to wonder if I did something wrong, Lord. If I did, Father God, I am so sorry, and I am repenting today to you, Lord. Let the words of my mouth order my steps to a place where I can begin to feel whole and complete again. I need you right now, Lord. I need you right now. In the name of Jesus, we pray…. Amen.

Opening my eyes, I stretched my arms above my head. I wanted to start my day off with prayer before I even got up. Yesterday, marks a full year since my life flipped upside down, and I needed strength. I have been trying to reach Phe Phe, but I was told by Mason that she was away on business.

The death of my aunt was sudden, and although I wasn't prepared for it, I am thankful that God allowed me to have some time with her. She made sure that I had something hot to eat every day and tried to motivate me. She was so happy that Phe Phe came into our lives and was more excited than I was when I won the dance hall contest.

I wonder if that is what allowed her to go to her sleep, knowing that I was going to be okay. She was a fighter, but living with her every day allowed me to see that she was tired. She had taken care of everyone her entire life and needed someone to take care of her. I was happy that she was finally resting in peace, but I wouldn't be human if I didn't admit to myself that I was hurt that she was gone.

My phone began to ring again, but I really wasn't in the mood to talk. Mason informed me that a letter came in regard to my case, and he wanted to open it together, but I was afraid to read it.

With my life going the way it was, I was not going to go anywhere, and I was beginning to become content with that.

Again, my phone rang, and it was starting to get on my nerves. I snatched the phone up off the counter and screamed, "HELLO!"

"Iyana, did I wake you?" Phe Phe asked.

"No Mami, I am okay. What's up?" I was so happy to hear from her that she didn't even know it.

"I am on my way over. Get dressed. I have some things that I need to show you."

"Are you alone, or is someone with you?" I had been avoiding Mason ever since the day we kissed. I hadn't seen or heard too much about Neka since the day I met him, but I refused to play seconds to anyone.

"No baby, I am alone."

I told her okay and hung up the phone. My heart began to beat uncontrollably in my chest. I couldn't take any more bad news. Wondering what she had to tell me, I got up off the couch and went into the bathroom to get myself together.

Finally, the Truth
Phe Phe

Quietly, I stood outside of Iyana's door, waiting for her to answer.

"Hey girl!" she called out with excitement in her voice and eyes. I hated leaving her alone on such an important day, but after I filled her in with all this news, I hoped that she would still look at me the same. I told myself on the flight back home that I was going to come clean and finally tell her everything, and I meant everything. I hated keeping secrets, but there was no one in this world that I trusted outside of the twins, and now her.

I knew the twins were loyal because we were intertwined together long before we ever met face to face. You see, when I was in jail, Michael came to visit me as my legal counsel. I never hired an attorney, so I didn't know what the hell the guard was talking about, but hey, if someone wanted to represent me, I was up for it.

Once seated across from each other, Michael informed me that he too was HIV positive, infected by Jason as well. He helped Jason save his brother from being deported. They got to know each other, and soon after, they were involved in a full-fledged relationship. It wasn't until Jason stopped frequenting Jamaica as much as he used to that Michael found out about me.

He actually found out that he was HIV positive a few months before I received my diagnosis, so that is why Jason didn't flinch when I told him mine. When word got back to Jamaica that Jason was murdered by his wife for giving her HIV, he had to come out to save me.

First, he didn't know that Jason liked women. He didn't even know about Jason's children with his ex-wife. So, when he came across me, Boo-Boo the Fool that allowed Jason to get me to change my gender, living as both the man and woman that he wanted all under one roof, Michael was beyond confused.

Once I unveiled everything to him, the twins did everything in their power to ensure that I did not rot in prison. If deportation was going to allow me to prevent that, then I was with it.

Softly, I closed the door behind me and placed my purse down on Iyana's table. The sound of Bob Marley's "No Woman No Cry" came from the radio in the living room. Iyana was in the kitchen, pouring us some tea to drink.

My hands were sweating so badly. Once she was seated, I handed her the manila envelope.

"What is this?"

Her hands shook as she took it from me, waiting for an answer.

I already told myself I wasn't going to say anything until she looked over everything. It was all in there: the transcription of the wiretapping that we had placed on the law firm's lines, conversations between Bradley and his uncle, discussing Iyana extensively, even a conversation about how Mr. Hinkle, who had set her parents up to be hit by the car that killed them. Apparently, Mr. Hinkle hated that not only was a nigger was elected partner, but a foreign one at that, who walked around like his shit didn't stink. He set out to make Iyana's father pay, literally. The twins and I even included statements from all of Iyana's bank accounts and documentation of everything she owned in the US, from her vehicles to the deed to her home.

The paperwork from the ICE department from the statement that Bradley provided them, directly stating that she had a drug habit, and a copy of the phone records of the anonymous call that they received, informing them of Iyana's charge.

There were pictures of Bradley with Daisy and other women going in and out of Iyana's home. There was also footage of me with Bradley, on the night of the 4th of July, with his hands all over me.

Then, I took pictures of how I left the crime scene afterwards. With the two of them lying on top of each other, naked and bludgeoned to death.

The last thing the folder contained was a picture of me, the old me as Felix.

It took her a while to go through everything, reading certain pages in depth, while turning her head away from the gruesome sights. She was full of emotion, crying silently as she flipped through the story of her life. Once she reached the picture of Felix, she picked it up with a look of confusion on her face.

"Do you have a twin? Who is this?"

I grabbed both of Iyana's hands in mine and looked her directly in the eyes. "No love," I answered. "I do not have a brother. I was the only son that my parents had. I am really a transgender woman."

Iyana pulled her hands back, covering her mouth, shaking her head. "What do you mean you are transgender? You are not a woman? You look so real!" I filled in the pieces and told her everything. She stared at me in disbelief. "You were the one that killed Bradley? Di- di- did you have sex with him?"

"No! Of course not, I have AIDS Iyana. I am not having sex with anyone. Please, before you judge me, let me show you why I have been so secretive, why I am living in constant fear. Just let me show you where I came from, so you can understand how it was so easy for me to get caught up in my situation."

At first, she looked at me with such disgust on her face that I did not think that she was going to go anywhere with me, but after a moment, she stood up and said softly, "Let's go."

Gully Queens

Iyana

Even though I was nervous, I had to appear strong for the sake of my friend. Following Phe Phe, I held onto the gate and used it for balance as we entered through the tiny hole.

We hopped down the sewer and walked inside. At first, the men appeared to be on guard as we entered their home, but once Phe Phe started talking and calling each one of them by name, the tension began to dissipate.

It was hard for me to wrap my mind around all the information that Phe Phe gave me in the last 24 hours. Not only was she a transgender woman, but she used to live underground in a sewer. Even though we were in a gully with the roaches and rats, these men made a makeshift home out of it. Quietly, I listened and didn't say anything.

These men had built an entire community down here with no support from the surrounding neighborhood or the government, and that impressed me the most. They had created a functioning establishment with everyone playing a role in making it run. There was a room full of makeshift beds made out of sheets, carpet, and pillows. There was a kitchen area where meals were created in pots and cooked on top of a wood-burning fire. Each person had their own heavy duty plastic bucket with a lid to prevent any insects and or rodents from getting to their own personal food items and toiletries. These men even established a wash and fold area where the girly men hung their feminine clothes out to dry on a clothesline to the left side of the gully, and the rest of them hung their stuff up to the right.

There was even a makeshift dressing room where the girly men sat together and did their hair and makeup.

The gully went on for miles and miles. Each block was utilized for something different, such as cooking, cleaning, and finances. But at the end of the day, the freedom that we had as individuals to live under a real roof was taken from them because of the fear of what someone may do to them.

I grabbed Phe Phe's hand, stopping her as she continued to walk through the maze, introducing me to people, pointing out specific landmarks. There was fresh running water coming through a broken fire hydrant that was used as a shower area and other places she had special memories that were dear to her.

A lot of the men down there had partnered up with a mate and established their own sense of an immediate family. As Phe Phe explained, it made their time down there a little easier, but for Phe Phe, she was all alone. They used to tell her that she was so pretty, that if she was ever able to become a girl for real, her life would be different.

Well, she did, and from what I can see, she was still living with the same fears, hurt, and pain that she may have had as a man.

When she turned around to face me, there were tears running down her cheeks. I tried to wipe her face, but she pulled back away from me.

"It's okay, Iyana," she said. "These tears, I am not ashamed for anyone to see them. I need the other gully queens to see me and know that life does go on. It's all about what you do with your time that will make a difference in someone else's life. I was born a gay man, and after a full-blown sex change, I am now a woman. I am dying of AIDS. According to my naysayers, I have a one-way ticket to hell. And that may be correct, but I still think the God I believe in is a God of love and will never forsake his children. No, I am not perfect, but I do try.

"The moment I met you, Iyana, I knew that you were greatness. Hearing your circumstances made life seem unfortunate for you, and it could have been, if you didn't have any help. I heard your need and did not hesitate to help you. I didn't know you from Adam. You could have just said thank you and went along with your life, and that would have been okay as well, but you didn't. You stayed and became the best sister-friend that I have ever had in my entire life.

"I was at a place of giving up at that moment, but Iyana, you breathed life into me. I needed that from you. Seeing you succeed makes me know that God has complete control and the final say. So, I want to thank you from the bottom of my heart. I can never get that back, and I would not have known if I didn't believe in you and took that chance."

The pep that I was about to give her was mediocre compared to those beautiful words that just escaped her lips. Now, I was crying like a baby. I know everyone around us was staring with a look of confusion, but it's okay if no one else understands. As long as we understand and hold down each other, there wasn't anything else that one could or needed to ask for.

"Thank you for sharing your story with me, Phe, for real," I told her. "I needed to see this. I thought I was brave, tackling my deportation the way that I did, but that was chump change compared to you, having to make a decision for yourself and move down here. That was beautiful and brave."

"Thank you for being you, Iyana. Do you still look at me differently?"

Forcefully, I pulled back to look her dead into her eyes. "No, baby. You will always just be Ms. Phoebe "Phe Phe" Godfrey to me. The best big sister that money could ever buy. Now, let's get out of here," I said, drying my eyes. "I am hungry and ready to eat! Let me take you out for dinner, my treat!"

Nodding her head, Phe Phe giggled and pulled me in close. Then, she went around and said her good-byes to everyone before protectively guided me out of the storm drain.

Can't Run Forever

Phe Phe

Reaching down, I helped Iyana maintain her balance as we exited the gully. I tried to study her face to see if she had any form of reservation for coming out with me today. If she looked at me differently after discovering that I used to be one of the men down there, that I used to be ashamed of who I was.

Iyana must have felt my worries because she stopped me before we reached the main road and embraced me with so much love. Tears, filled with love, confusion, pain, and joy, streamed down my face.

It was almost dark, and I was ready to take Iyana to the final part of our trip. I was going to take her to my home. I needed her to know that I trusted her wholeheartedly and that I would forever have her back, even if she decided to go home to Florida.

Loosening the clenching grip, I had on Iyana's hand; a feeling of peace came over me. This was the first time that I shared my story and had an opportunity to show someone that generally loves me how I used to live. It was rush hour in New Kingston, and the traffic on Trafalgar Road was at a standstill.

Weaving our way through the vehicles, I was so busy trying to ensure that we were good, I didn't notice the three youths watching us and approaching us from the opposite direction.

We were almost on the other side of the street when the group finally caught up with us. The smile that was planted on my face quickly dissipated when I noticed that they were not trying to get around us, they wanted us. Well, not us. It was me who they wanted.

It didn't take me long to recognize the youth that stood directly before me. I had seen his face many times in the photos that used to decorate my home back in D. C. It was David, Jason's son.

We stood there for what felt like an eternity and stared each other down. The pace of my heart sped up tremendously, but I was not going to let them know that they put any fear into my heart.

Slightly turning my head, I looked at Iyana and mouthed the words, "I love you," but quickly turned back to face my aggressor.

"Mi did a luk Fi yuh an kno seh mi wud a fine yuh round yah suh. Wi fine yuh. Now wi a guh kill yuh!"

Grabbing me by my hair, Jason punched me in my face over and over again. I pushed Iyana away, screaming at her, "Iyana, run! Gyal run a nuh luk back!"

Attempting to swing back didn't make any sense because his goon squad quickly grabbed each of my arms as he continued to hit me. A crowd began to form around us as they screamed out and called me all kinds of names.

The man holding my left arm pulled out a knife and handed it to David. All the fight I had in my body was gradually going away as I watched the knife coming closer to my throat. He leaned in so close to me that I was able to inhale the sour scent of the rum he had consumed earlier.

The last thing I remembered was hearing him whisper into my ear, "Now yuh a guh ded."

All of a sudden, everything went black around me as I felt him quickly pierced my throat. I pray Iyana got away, but I know this is it for me. After everything that I have been through, I'm tired and ready to rest.

"Can't run forever," I whispered to myself as I took my final breath.

Iyana

Shaking, I watched as they beat, kicked, and stabbed my friend's crumpled body, laying on the ground. The gang was screaming at Phe Phe, calling her a man, a batty bwoy, causing the crowd in the street to turn into an angry mob.

"We nah wan nuh one of yuh in our town," they yelled.

Now, it just wasn't the original gang of young men beating my friend, but it was men and women kicking and screaming at her. Some people had sticks, some people even took off their shoes, beating and dragging her lifeless body.

I didn't see where the fire came from, but after I heard the gunshots ring out and connect with my friend's head, I knew I needed to get out of there and fast. If they could do that to a person that *appeared* to be a woman without even verifying that she was really a man, what the hell would they do to me? I caught my breath and ran down the road. I needed to get to Mason or Michael quickly. Again, in my life, another person that I trusted was taken from me. Who was going to protect me now?

Two Weeks Later

Peace at Last

Iyana

Sitting inside the church in the front row, the pain inside my chest would not subside. Every night since it happened, I have had the recurring nightmare of the horrific massacre of my friend. When I returned with Michael and Mason to claim her body, I didn't even recognize her.

Collapsed beside her remains, I began to bawl. It was a sound that came from the pit of my stomach, one that I had never heard before.

Kneeling beside me, Mason tried to calm me down.

"Baby, it's over," he whispered to me. I stared up at him in disbelief.

"How can they get away with this?!" I screamed out loud to no one in particular. "Why is she still out here, not even covered up?"

"Shhh, my love. Her family disowned her since she had the surgery, so the police considered her to be Jane Doe. It is unfortunate circumstances, but until the island of Jamaica catches up with the rest of the world, there will be others left out on the concrete alone, just like her."

Her body was in pieces. The police informed us that after I left someone in the mob ran over her with their car, not once, or twice, but three damn times!

I had to look away because I could not bear seeing her like this. I wanted to remember the person that I met, the person I had grown to love like my sister, and in turn, she had loved me. I knew it sounded crazy, but I didn't even want to remember her as Felix. That is not the person that I knew. It didn't matter to me at that point that she used to be a man, or that she was a murderer. I didn't care that she had AIDS and was dying a slow death every day. The only thing that mattered to me was that she loved and treated me like family. I would never stop loving her.

It wasn't until that moment when I had to look away that I realized how ironic and small this island really is. Right here, in the middle of Trafalgar Road where my best friend was murdered, was right in front of same hotel where my parents lived while pregnant with me.

My heartbeat quickened, and I suddenly I felt lightheaded. As my body began to quiver, Mason wrapped his arms around.

"Baby, I will never leave you," he said, kissing the top of my head.

We were the only ones at the church service. Besides my friend, Mary, and Michael, Mason and I were the only ones that cared enough to see Phe Phe be laid to rest. I now understood why Emmett till's mother held his funeral with an open casket because she wanted the world to see the devastation that was bestowed upon her son. I wanted to do the same thing, but knowing the type of person Phe was, I knew that she would not be going for that.

I bowed my head and said a prayer for Phe Phe, my aunt, my parents, I even said one for Bradley. Even though God had literally taken everyone that I love away from me, he has blessed me with the wisdom that everything is going to be okay.

I felt someone's presence on my left side of me. I opened my eyes to be greeted by the warmness of Mason's smile.

"How are you holding up?" he asked.

I smiled a weak smile and squeezed his hand. "I am just happy that I had the money to be able to give my friend the service that she deserved," I told him. "I will be okay. I don't know if I will be able to get on stage again without her, but I will be fine. How are you feeling? I know that Phe Phe held a special place in your heart as well."

Kissing my cheek, Mason reached into the inside pocket of his suit and pulled out two white envelopes addressed to me.

"What is this?" I asked, confused as he handed me the paper. I already paid for Phe Phe's cremation and memorial service. Even though only a few of us will have memories of her, I wanted her to have the best, but I knew that these could not be bills.

Mason nodded, encouraging me to read as tears filled his eyes. I did not think that I could take any more bad news, but I took a deep breath and unfolded the letter.

Shocked, I was not ready to see that it was a letter addressed to me from Phe Phe. My hands began to shake as I read the letter aloud.

"My dearest friend Iyana,

I first want to thank you for teaching me how to love again. I did not think that I was capable of sharing that emotion again, but you did everything in your power to make sure that I felt it coming from you. If you are reading this, then that means I am dead. I am not HIV positive, I have full-blown AIDS, contracted to me by my late-husband, Jason. Hopefully, by now, I have told you the truth about my status, so if I haven't at least now you know.

I have been dying slowly, and I have grown very tired and weak. I am so happy that I was able to meet you and look at life from a different perspective. You gave me something to live for. Because of this, I feel that it is only right that in the event anything happens to me, I leave you everything that I own. My house in Beverly Hills and everything within its walls, my two cars, and my motorbikes.

I also leave you with my entire estate and all the money in my accounts. I am worth about $180,000 USD. It's the law of the land. Bradley stole from you and took all your money and possessions, and I am giving it back. I love you, my Yankee sister. Keep your head up.

Thank you again for loving me.

— Phe

August 6, 2014

Epilogue
Iyana

Immediately after the funeral, Mason drove to Phe Phe's beautiful home. There was a winding driveway that led you up to the property and palm trees literally everywhere. Her home was so beautiful that I still needed to pinch myself to know that I was not dreaming.

The second letter that I received was from the US Department of Customs and Enforcement. After all the fighting that Mason, Michael, and Phe Phe had done in the name of freeing me, I could legally go back to America as a Permanent Resident. It has been over a year now since I was forced to come back home to the tiny island of Jamaica and learn how to love me.

Now, Mason pushed the papers across the table for me to sign. It was official: a Belizean couple, the Lockwood's, just purchased the home that once belonged to my parents, the home that I grew up in, and then, the home that Bradley tore apart, trying to get rich quick and including me in the process of elimination. Now, I needed to erase the property from my memories and come up with a new summer property for Mason and me to share.

It was bittersweet, stepping back into the house that I used to call my own. When I first landed on Jamaica, I called and begged that fool Bradley to send me my precious clothes, my belongings. I walked the halls with a look of disgust on my face. Bradley did everything in his power to wipe away any traces of my parents and I, but that was okay. All the renovations that he did made the property worth more and a buyer's dream. It didn't take me long at all to obtain an offer, but once I heard the sing-song accent of Mrs. Lockwood, I knew that was a sign from my mother telling me that they were the ones for our home.

Even though I was happy to be able to travel across seas on my own accord, I was about ready to go back home. I only had one more stop, and that was to thank Detective Smith. If it weren't for him the damage that Bradley has reeked upon trusting Caribbean women would have never been noticed, and the girl that Phe Phe caught him with would have probably been his next victim.

"Are you ready, Mrs. Eubanks? Hearing him say my name like that ran chills up and down my spine.

"That is not my name yet, Mr. Eubanks, but I LOVE LOVE LOVE the way it sounds on your tongue."

Biting my lower lip, I leaned over and kissed Mason fully on the lips.

"Yes baby, I am ready to get out of here, and go home. WE have more lives to save."

Reviews

If you enjoy this story, please leave a review.
This is how others will know to take the time
and read a novel from the pen of Ni'cola!
Thank you so much!
Just click on the following link:
http://amzn.to/1IYcbT0

Introducing

Ni'cola Mitchell

Striving to inject her unique flair into the realm of contemporary fiction, Award-Winning, Best-Selling author and blogger, Ni'cola Mitchell enter the literary scene with one main objective: To Stimulate Your Mind, One Word at a Time. Through her independent publishing company NCM Publishing, Ni'cola published numerous titles which have been featured on various best-selling lists throughout the country. Much of her work revolves around complex relationship issues and Mitchell's compulsive desire to see women overcome challenges.

Originally from Kingston, Jamaica, she currently resides in North Las Vegas, Nevada with her two daughters Destani and Diamond. Ni'cola is also the CFO of Obsessive Soul Media and Co-Founder of the Baltimore Urban Book Festival. She sits on the board of the Miss Black Collegiate USA Scholarship Pageant and manages the pageant's Author Pavilion. She is also a primary panel member for the State of Black Parent Conference. Ni'cola is also the Celebrity Brand Ambassador for Premier

Hair. She is a contributing writer for Urbania Magazine and FeedLynks, the Urban News Network. Ni'cola is a Strategic Partner for the California's Women's Conference and is also a 2014 Blogger's Week Ambassador. She holds a bachelor's degree of Science in Business Management and is currently pursuing a master's in film.

Over and Over Again was featured in the top ten by EDC Creations Recommended Reading List the 2009 fall season under Mainstream Fiction and Women's Fiction. Ni'cola was nominated Self-Published Author of the Year with the African American Literary Award Show for 2010, 2011, and 2012. Her short story "The Forbidden Rain" was featured in the Between the Sheets anthology which won 2011 Anthology of the Year with the African American Literary Award Show. Ni'cola's distinctive writing talent has led her to become a featured columnist for Urb Society Magazine, and a nominee for the 2014 I Am a Diva, literary awards. With her outstanding representation of Las Vegas' African American community, Ni'cola Mitchell was featured in the second edition of Who's Who in Black Las Vegas. As well as being an author, Nicola is also a motivational speaker and literary consultant, which allowed her to become the recipient of the 2013 Queen that Rocks Award, from the Heal a Woman to Heal a Nation Conference. Ni'cola was also the

2015 Upward Bound Honoree award, presented by the University of Nevada Las Vegas.

Currently, she is touring across the country, speaking about the importance of going after your dreams and overcoming obstacles, and how to self-publish your book successfully. When she isn't writing, Mitchell loves to spend time with her family and volunteers as a mentor for youth activities. To find out more check out.

www.nicolacmitchell.com.

For any questions or comments
Please email us at
info@fromthepenofnicola.com
Also
Follow Ni'cola on social media!
www.facebook.com/AuthorMsNicola
www.twitter.com/MsNicola
www.instagram.com/Mz_Nicola

Other Titles from the pen of Ni'cola:

Over and Over Again

The Appetizer,
When You're Not His Main Course

"Forbidden Rain" Between the Sheets

Twisted

A Cold Piece

He's My Favorite Mistake

Love Don't Walk Away People Do

Beautiful Liar

Pum Pum

He's My Favorite Mistake 2

Defiance of Chance